I0760719

Forced by his publisher to deliver a fresh manuscript by the end of the year, author Rick Rooney retreats to a secluded cottage in the West of Ireland in search of inspiration.

After a night of dabbling with a spirit board at the local pub, strange events unfold at the cottage, while a menacing figure stalks outside.

When Rick digs deeper into the area's dark history, he makes a chilling discovery. But has Rick disturbed an ancient evil, and who, or what, is stalking him now?

NP CUNNIFFE

The Weejee Man

First published by ScaryBooks 2023

First edition

ISBN: 978-1-9164585-1-2

This book was professionally typeset on Reedsy.
Find out more at reedsy.com

Contents

Foreword

The spirit board in this book, referred to as 'weejee', is not based on any particular product, brand, or design. The chosen spelling is simply a local adaptation reflecting the pronunciation in the West of Ireland, where the events in the book occur. While spirit or talking boards are known by various names like 'wee-ja', 'we-ja', 'weed-ja', etc., the selection of 'weejee' is solely influenced by the local context.

△

For a list of **CONTENT WARNINGS,** skip to the back matter. Read, or do not read, at your own risk.

You have been warned.

Preface

The following introduction is a commissioning editor's email to his publisher shortly before his death. Subsequent emails appear later to compliment the flow of the narrative and have undergone a very light copyedit. Other auxiliary files, including letters, have been included in their entirety where possible, and are similarly ordered and copyedited. We, the publisher, have made this decision purely for the reader's benefit.

Rick Rooney's recovered manuscript, including chapter titles, is presented in its entirety where possible.

I

Pierce, 2020

Email from Pierce Rowlandson to Julia Crouch

From: pierce rowlandson <pierce.rowlandson@caxtonpublishing.com>
Sent: Wednesday, January 1, 2020 1:50 PM
To: julia.crouch@caxtonpublishing.com
Subject: Rick

Julia,

You won't believe what's happened to Rick this time.

I received a phone call from a hospital on New Year's Eve. I was home, as usual, casually winding up the Twitter trolls, Shirley purring in my lap, when an unfamiliar number appeared on my screen. A young male voice informed me he was phoning from Portiuncula Hospital in Ballinasloe. I'd never heard of those places before. I could only assume Ireland. He said a man named Rick had recently been taken into intensive care.

I'd been waiting to hear from Rick for months. He'd been quieter than usual. He had said he was planning to undergo a 'Digital Detox.' I'd sent him emails and left him several voicemails, but he never phoned back. I can't imagine someone willingly giving up their phone, or any devices, for that matter. Anyway, I'd hoped he'd been busy working on something new, as part of this mad detox. Perhaps he'd followed my advice and taken a holiday, found some much-needed inspiration. Maybe he was doing his detox in Ireland. But a phone call from a strange-sounding hospital wasn't the call I was expecting.

"He's not speaking," the nurse said. I wondered if this young man might be handsome, like in those hospital dramas. Sorry, but I don't get out much! "He doesn't even have a phone," the nurse continued. "We managed to find your business card in his wallet – I hope you don't mind. But apart from that, we couldn't find any other contact information. He has a journal with him but, to be honest, his writing is so poor it's barely legible."

He explained that Rick was found lying in a graveyard unconscious with extensive injuries. I struggled to listen to what he was saying; I could only think about the journal Rick was found carrying – and the nurse. Was it a full draft of a new book? The result of this detox? Had he churned out a bestselling novel at last? I have to admit, I was curious. And, as commissioning editor, it's my responsibility to ensure it gets published and I hit my annual targets, as I'm sure you would agree, Julia.

"Does he have any family members we can contact?" the nurse asked.

"I can check," I said, though of course I wanted to be his first visitor. I needed that manuscript in my hands.

"Well, we'll keep looking," the nurse said, a hint of fatigue in his voice.

"When can I visit?"

"Visiting times are between two and four, and five and seven. But just to let you know, he's not very responsive. I know it can be a shock at first, but he's been like this for weeks, so don't take it personally. He doesn't seem to be suffering any memory loss, so he should still recognise you. We can only assume some psychological trauma has occurred. And please don't push him to speak. We don't want to overexert him."

"Can I visit tomorrow?" I asked.

"He's stable for now, so, yes, you should be able to visit tomorrow. He's in St Joseph's Ward now. Room twelve. It might be good for him to see a familiar face."

Shirley didn't seem too pleased when I left her with the neighbour. "It'll only be a day or two," I promised. Her green eyes glared suspiciously. It was a promise I was fully committed to keeping. I didn't want to linger too long in Ireland, and certainly not in a depressing ward in some hospital. Get the story and get back to work.

I arrived at the hospital this afternoon, determined to be Rick's first visitor. I struggled to remember the last time I'd visited a hospital. Of course, I visit the vet for Shirley, but I'm inclined to stay away from hospitals if I can. And yet the pale green walls and sickly beige floors seemed familiar, as if I'd been here before. I suppose I see hospitals on TV, when I'm not drowning in all the manuscripts flooding our inboxes. I like the occasional *Doctors* or *Nurse Jackie*. And especially that one with George Clooney. And don't get me started on *Call the Midwife*.

The air in the hospital atrium was heavy. Stagnant. And a smell like old, sweaty bedsheets permeated the place. Even the overpowering disinfectant on the floors couldn't mask it. And strangely, above it all, the sickly smell of ripened bananas. My stomach churned. The coffee I'd had while driving didn't help.

I glanced up at the board. St Joseph's Ward was on the third floor. Would Rick recognise me? Could I make him talk?

The last time I saw him was at his own book launch. He's not the type of author to meet for a coffee. He was with Rachel. I didn't stay long, of course. I'm not exactly a social butterfly, am I?

I reached the third floor, my stomach jittery. I checked the door numbers, continuing down the corridor until I reached room twelve. It was quiet in this corner of the hospital, and my footsteps echoed on the glossy floor.

I neared the last door on the right. I wondered what Rick would look like. Would his head be disfigured in some way? The nurse had said it was a head injury when I pushed for the details. What had happened at the graveyard?

Of course, the door was locked. It's not yet two o'clock. I was so focused on getting here ASAP, I didn't even notice the time. Still, I peered through the glass, trying to get a good look. Unfortunately, Rick's bed was curtained off. It looked like his was the only bed in the room.

So here I am in the busy hospital café, having a decaf coffee. I should be in the office Monday, with a shiny new manuscript in hand. Quite literally too. Not a bad start to the year!

I feel like an amateur journalist again, writing this. Maybe that's why this email is so long; perhaps the young ambitious journalist inside me has awoken after a four-decade slumber. But this could be something, Julia. It's been a long time since we've had a bestseller, and the pressure has never been higher.

It's almost two, so I better get going. I'd been enjoying my moment on my laptop with my coffee, documenting this wild excursion, despite all the noise here. I'll keep you posted on Rick and the manuscript. Who knows, maybe you'll get a sneak peek!

Regards,

Pierce

PS a threat to terminate an author's contract never fails!

II

Rick, 2019

The Graveyard

I suppose I should start where it all ends: the graveyard.

It was a clear but chilly autumn afternoon. The Eve of Samhain, to be precise. The sun almost blinded me as I drove along the old roads. I was still amazed at how green the countryside could be, no matter the time of year, even after spending my entire childhood here. A stark difference to the view from our shoebox flat in London. The roads were wet, as is usually the case in Ireland, the trees a dazzling mix of browns, reds and golds, even through my prescription blue-light-blocking sunglasses.

I was glad to have come home, although it wasn't exactly a choice; my editor, Pierce, practically forced me to take a holiday and find inspiration, threatening to terminate my contract if I didn't deliver by the end of the year. Rachel agreed and found a small cottage near a secluded lake in my home county, suggesting a return to my roots might inspire something – although I fear Pierce went behind my back and persuaded her.

An old, ruined tower upon a hill appeared in the corner of my windscreen. The graveyard was snugged away behind the ancient abbey, shadowed by the crumbling tower. I swerved the rented car onto a narrow path and parked it beneath the looming branches of an oak, just outside the gate.

I turned off the engine and rolled down the window for some fresh air. The car had become stuffy after the few hours of driving from the airport. I could smell damp autumn leaves that'd been stewing all day in the sun.

It was a quiet corner of Ireland; quite possibly the quietest and most serene spot one might visit. Green fields rolled far into the distance, too far for the eye to see, promising plenty of space for the ever-growing number of residents. The graveyard had expanded quite considerably since I'd been here last. Generation after generation of my family were buried here, including my parents; the Mulrooneys probably occupied most of the graves. My father once told me I should buy my own plot here. That was a while ago now.

My phone flashed from the passenger seat. I had received some new voice messages, most likely from Pierce. I turned it face down; the last thing I needed was Pierce lecturing in my ear. "It's nothing more than short-term writer's block," he would say when I eventually answered the phone. "All writers go through it. Just take a break, go somewhere quiet. Rest your mind. You'd be amazed what boredom can do for creativity. And don't forget your deadline!"

But it wasn't writers' block – I hated that term anyway. Nobody says 'surgeon's block' or 'carpenters' block' – a job is a job, and writing is a job that needs doing too, whatever the mood. I just didn't want to. I didn't want to get up and work, even if that involved only a couple of steps to the desk at the end of my bed. I'd lost all motivation recently. But Pierce doesn't believe it. Or he doesn't want to believe it.

"It's been six months," he'd reminded me, and, later, "ten months." But perhaps I needed a break. A *real* break, not a writing retreat. I'd written eleven books for Caxton & co – how many did they want? When would they give me a break?

I rolled up the window, as the air was getting chilly. It was also getting dark. Shadows stretched across the graves, headstones black against the reddening October sky. I'd forgotten how quickly it darkened this time of year. I turned the key in the ignition and reversed the car down the hill, deciding to return another day. I had a whole week to visit.

Glancing in the rear-view mirror, I glimpsed my pale reflection, before averting my gaze quickly. I prefer not to see the physical toll these sleepless months had taken. Only in my mid-thirties and already showing heavy lines on my forehead and flecks of grey in my hair. There's nothing admirable to behold in that reflection.

I secured my glasses and pulled down my cap.

I'd hoped to get a decent night's sleep at the cottage without the help of medication. Maybe my body would finally succumb to it out here in the quiet countryside. I pressed down on the accelerator, excited at the prospect. But sleep wouldn't come to me at the cottage. In fact, I haven't enjoyed a full night's sleep since.

Black Lake Cottage

It was shortly after five when I found the cottage, although I would have found it a lot sooner had I not made a detour to the old family home. I sat outside in the car far longer than I'd intended, hoping nobody was inside.

Not much had changed, although I suppose it had only been a few years since their passing. The garden looked tidier, the hedges perfectly trimmed, the grass an acceptable height. My parents had struggled to keep it under control in their later years, while Rachel and I were settling into our first flat in London. I remember everything overgrown, ivy climbing up the walls to the roof. Now all the ivy had been torn down, leaving the walls awkwardly bare, naked and pink. The windows looked double-glazed, black plastic frames replacing the rotting wood I was familiar with while growing up here. It was hard to keep the place warm in the winter, even when they brought in the central heating.

After a good hour sitting in the car, and no sign of movement inside, I decided nobody was home. I couldn't help but have a little nose around. If anyone asked, I'd just say I was a tourist. We sometimes had tourists, mainly American, asking if they could take photos of the farm, the tractors and the hay. I'd thought they were nuts, but I suppose they were after something authentic.

The afternoon had grown colder, so I donned my favourite fingerless gloves and wrapped a woolly scarf around my neck, keeping my glasses in place. I crossed the narrow road, not bothering to lock the car. The smell of damp straw greeted me. An unlit pumpkin, which I hadn't noticed from the car, was nestled under the hedge. Clearly nobody was home, or a candle would be lit for Halloween. It was only then that I saw the black cutouts, of witches flying on brooms, glued to the windows.

I continued past the hedges and around the side of the house, into the backyard. It didn't appear that the farm buildings were used. No tractors or trailers occupied the sheds; bikes and tricycles lay scattered across the ground. In the dark of a shed sat a large mound of turf.

I wondered how many children were in this family. My parents had said the size of the house, with its two bedrooms, was the reason I was an only child.

Strange that the smell of straw still lingered. It was even stronger than the earthy smell of turf. Maybe it had seeped into the very walls of the house and sheds.

I headed in the direction of the larger sheds, careful not to muddy my shoes. The doors were open, but the sheds were completely empty inside. *A waste,* I thought. Even for these apparent non-farmers. They were probably from the city, and didn't know what to do with all the space. I was surprised they even kept turf. I suppose some traditions never die out here.

The smell of damp hay and straw intensified as I walked. The trees became sparse the further I went, revealing field upon field that continued down into the vale. I'd spent many summers in those fields, running after my father in his tractor and mower, tripping over the freshly-turned tufts, being a nuisance. I was never really an outdoors person, but I always enjoyed watching the long grass being scythed and turned into mountainous piles of hay. And then, of course, I'd be launching myself into it and undoing my father's good work, and I definitely deserved more than a clip around the ear for that.

I was so lost in thought that I almost didn't register the figure standing inside one of the sheds. Seconds later I stopped, realising what I'd just seen, wondering if they had seen me. Surely they would have said something to a trespasser on their property? But, as I stood motionless, I couldn't hear anything. Perhaps they were busy with something and hadn't seen or heard me.

Not wanting to snoop any more, I took a couple of steps backwards, clearing my throat.

"Hello?" I said.

There was no reply. They didn't move. They looked incredibly dark through my sunglasses. Nervous, I took them off and peered into the shed. The figure wasn't a person at all. It was just a rake resting against the back wall, a coat hanging from the tines. I breathed a sigh of relief.

My father was always putting up some kind of scarecrow around the fields. On Halloween, I'd find a figure below my bedroom window, facing the road. A few years later, I realised it was just an old coat and hat upon a rake or hayfork. I think it was to ward off trick-or-treaters, or maybe it was there to prevent *me* from trick-or-treating. Whatever the case, I would stay inside all day, peering out at the figure from my bedroom window and well into the night, my hand gripping the curtain, wondering if it would move. The coat sometimes fluttered, but in my head I saw the figure rotate fully, a smile spreading wide to reveal a mouth packed with razor-like teeth. That never happened, of course, but I never went outside until it was taken down. And it always did, before I woke the next day. Sometimes I imagined it walking off down the road just before dawn. Maybe it was those experiences that turned me into a horror writer.

I heard the faint hum of a car. The house and farmyard were pleasantly secluded, thick coniferous trees sheltering it from the road, but it was still possible to hear the odd car motoring past. I stepped away from the shed and made my way back to the rental.

△

I turned left after the monastery, as per the route in my memory, and continued driving down the narrow road that sliced through the dense forest. I knew the turn-off to the lake was along this road, I just didn't know where; I'd never been there before. I considered turning on the sat nav. Then I glanced at the book on the dashboard. *Turning Off: Your Guide to a Successful Digital Detox* by Bob Newport. I'd only read a couple of chapters, but I knew cutting out distractions was what I needed on this trip. Besides, I doubt the sat-nav would have picked up this back road anyway.

Finally, after crawling at a slow speed, I spotted it, almost obscured by the forest.

Branches brushed the sides of the car; I hoped they wouldn't scratch the paintwork. A road turned off to the right – possibly back to the main road – so I continued straight ahead. After a couple of minutes, the lake came into view, a dark pool within a hollow, largely enclosed by the forest. I turned right and saw the cottage, nestled amongst the tall thick trees and overlooking the water.

I reverse-parked the car by a sign that read *Black Lake* and studied the cottage through the windscreen: my little abode for the next week. At least it looked little from the outside, and in the shape of a beehive hut. The smooth, slated roof gleamed in the headlights. The flat white walls looked new, covering the original stonework. The cottage looked quite snug, actually. Perfect for a week, or maybe even two. Perhaps a relaxing break was exactly what I needed.

I stuffed the book and phone into my bag and got out of the car, excitement tingling in my stomach. I wasn't sure if it was the lateness of the day, or the shadows of the forest, but the water was the colour of charcoal. Hence the name, I suppose. It was also deathly quiet, as if all noise was swallowed by the forest.

A rumble sounded from my stomach. I checked my watch: it had just gone five. I hadn't eaten since Heathrow Airport. I knew there were a couple of pubs around, but serving dinner? Resisting the urge to search on my phone (what would Bob Newport say?!), I turned the engine and lights off and locked the car, before retrieving my suitcase and hurrying towards the cottage, hunger quickening my step. Perhaps I'd find something to nibble inside – did landlords leave such treats for their guests? I hurried towards the cottage, my feet crunching on loose stone, before searching my pockets for my phone for some light. I'd decided I would only use my phone in an emergency, or if I needed the light.

As I fumbled for my phone, everything around me was suddenly bleached in a blinding white light, making me wince.

It was so bright, I had to hold my arm over my eyes. I struggled to keep them open, but the source of the light seemed to be emanating from above the cottage door. A motion-detector light, perhaps.

Edging closer to the door, one arm held over my eyes, my knee banged something hard. A large pot was already toppling to the ground. I reached out to grasp it, dropping my suitcase. But I was too slow.

Crack.

I cursed as I dropped to my knees. The pot had shattered into many small fragments, and soil littered the stones. The pot that possibly hid the key for the front door, as the landlord's message had instructed. After searching on hands and knees, I felt cold metal beneath my fingers, hidden in the dirt. *Not the greatest start,* I thought. I'd have to buy a new pot. At least I'd banged into only one.

I blew the dirt from the key and reached for my case. The cottage door opened with a yawning creak, as if it hadn't been opened in years. A chill in the air made me shudder. I wondered how many guests had stayed here before. I hadn't read any reviews, or looked at any photos – I'd put my trust in Rachel. Besides, I had no way to search for reviews without using my phone.

I flicked the light switch. I was relieved to see a modest fireplace in the living room, and a wicker basket full of turf. The next thing I noticed was a mirror above the hearth, which was thankfully too dusty to show my reflection. All the same, I crossed the room and turned it around so I wouldn't have to worry. It wasn't that I was superstitious – as much as I yearned to see my parents again, I knew I never would – it's just I didn't want to see my tired reflection. Especially when I was trying to enjoy myself.

I turned around to take in the interior of the cottage properly. There seemed to be only a living area and a small kitchen at the front, which may have once been a bedroom. A compact, two-person settee and tiny coffee table made of mahogany took up most of the living room. Opposite was the kitchen, the cupboards and worktop made of wood. Both the living room and kitchen looked out towards the lake.

I closed my eyes, savouring this moment of quiet and calm. It reminded me of my parents' old kitchen, before it was revamped during their retirement and replaced with shiny, plastic surfaces that glared from every wall and corner. This cottage was homely. And then there was the fireplace, and the earthy smell of the turf. I had shied from the countryside for too long, but it was only then that I realised how much I'd missed rural life. The cottage wasn't my childhood home, but it was the closest I'd get. Rachel had chosen well.

I wheeled my suitcase down the hall, with thoughts of curling up by the fireplace with a warm drink forming in my head. There were two rooms at the rear of the cottage: one bedroom and a bathroom. A small writing desk sat snugly in the corner of the bedroom. The perfect place to write, if inspiration came. I'd packed a journal and numerous fancy felt-tip pens in case, but I wasn't going to force anything. I didn't want it to feel like work. Pierce could terminate my contract; I didn't care. I could always submit elsewhere.

I dropped my bag on the bed before checking for more mirrors. Relieved to see none, I found a stack of towels. I gathered a few in my arms, in case I would find another mirror.

Armed with towels, I opened the bathroom door. There was bound to be a mirror or two in here. Holding a towel before me, I made my way to the sink and felt around to locate a medicine cabinet. I flung the towel over it and glanced around. There was no other mirror in sight.

Relax, Rick, I told myself.

Leaving the rest of the towels in the bathroom, I made my way to the kitchen. It was small, with a round table and two chairs, but it had everything one might need: a kettle, microwave, tea bags and sugar, and even a fancy-looking coffee machine. I opened the cupboards in search of food, only to find plates and bowls. I was surprised to see a large bottle of brandy sitting on the countertop. I couldn't drink that on an empty stomach. Besides, I'd promised Rachel I wouldn't drink on this trip; it wasn't conducive to sleep, and the doctor had told me not to mix sleeping pills and alcohol anyway.

When I lifted the bottle, I found a note behind it. I sat down on a kitchen stool next to the countertop and turned it over. It was from Brian, the landlord.

Hello Rick,

I hope you found the cottage without too much difficulty. Please help yourself to a drink – I always find I need something strong after travelling. There's not much in the way of food I'm afraid, but I recommend checking out Castlestrange Lodge. It's less than a five-minute drive, or a twenty-minute walk if you cut through the forest. Food is served until eight. They do a lovely stew.

If you need anything, give me a shout. My mobile number is 0833073012. Please don't hesitate to call.

Enjoy your stay.

Brian

I pocketed the note and checked my watch – it had just gone

six. I should be able to make it with plenty of time, as the walk only took twenty minutes. I hid the bottle away in a cupboard, zipped my windbreaker jacket tight, and headed out.

Weejee

The walk didn't take twenty minutes as Brian had promised. That was mainly due to the darkness of the winding path through the forest. Luckily, I had my phone light to guide me. "It's not wise to walk the roads at night on the Eve of Samhain," my mother would tell me. It was that one night of the year when the dead had the power to return and walk amongst the living, before dancing on the hills to the fairy music until the dawn. I never believed in any of that anyway, even if it had fired my imagination. And it certainly wouldn't have stopped me from sneaking out, had I wanted to go trick-or-treating with the other kids. But I was too busy at home trying to watch every horror film that aired that night. I wonder if she'd really believed in all of that though, fairies and ghosts.

It was almost half-past six when I reached the main road. I knew where I was; the pub should only be a five- to ten-minute walk across the river. A small bridge glistened in the distance.

I crossed the bridge. The evening was quiet, so quiet I could only hear my breathing and my own footsteps. Long, twisted branches stretched above me. I'd never walked this road before, but I had driven along it at some point. I had a vague recollection of where the pub was situated, and its distance from the nearest village.

The road bent sharply to the left. I thought I saw lights glinting between the trees. I carried on. The trees became sparser, and I could make out a yellow wall from which a sign reading *Guinness* beamed. I found myself salivating at the thought of hot, hearty stew.

My legs were heavy and slow by the time I made it to the door; I wasn't used to walking so fast, having spent most of the previous months stuck inside a small flat, feeling sorry for myself. A sweet and smoky aroma escaped the building as I opened the door. I headed straight for the counter, hoping I didn't need to be seated first. A few men were perched upon stools, but I couldn't see a bartender. I checked my watch; a quarter to seven.

"What can I get you, young man?" came a voice with a thick, local accent.

Young man? I thought. I certainly didn't feel, or look, like a young man.

A woman in her late fifties or early sixties emerged from the back room behind the bar. She had a bright red face and grey-black hair, and a tea towel rested on her shoulder.

"Are you still serving?" I asked. She glanced at a clock between two high shelves.

"Just about," she said, even though it was only quarter to seven. Perhaps Brian had got the time wrong. "Take a seat and I'll be with ya."

I looked around, hoping to find a quiet corner. The last thing I wanted was to be forced to sit at the bar, in full view of everyone. A trio of men huddled around a circular table before a fire and, next to them, a small, unoccupied table for two. I pulled down my cap and headed towards it. I don't think the men noticed me, too engrossed in their conversation.

I hung my jacket on the back of the chair and sat down, keeping my scarf and cap on. I peered out from beneath the brim of the cap, surveying the room. A turf fire was lit in the hearth beside me, the source of the sweet smell. A large, rectangular mirror in a gilded frame hung above the mantelpiece, reflecting the interior of the pub. I averted my gaze quickly, instead scanning the bookshelf above me. There wasn't much to behold: a red hardback Bible, A-Z guidebooks, board games, a book of fairytales for children. I realised then that there were no books at the cottage, apart from Bob Newport. I knew I should have packed more, but I had wanted to give Bob's words my full attention.

A shadow fell across the table.

"Decided yet?" the bartender asked. I'd completely forgotten to look at the menu on the table. Without looking up, I asked, "I heard you serve nice stew?"

The woman placed her pink, wet hands on her hips. "Just lamb stew this evening,"

"Okay, perfect," I replied quickly.

"Anything to drink?"

"Just water."

When she left, my gaze returned to the bookshelf. It would be strange to start reading the Bible in a pub, and the A-Z guides would scream *tourist*. Stranger even to read a book for children. I kicked myself for not bringing *Digital Detox* with me; now I had nothing to look at. I resisted the burgeoning itch to pull out my phone; it wasn't even day two yet. I didn't even have my new journal and pens on me – not that I had anything to write. Still, I wanted to appear busy.

Should I text Rachel? I thought. *Just a simple "found the cottage"?* ~~But wasn't this a break from Rachel too? I hadn't told her~~

~~that, of course, but didn't I want to get away from her? Escape from her? Wasn't that something I wanted?~~

[Note to editor: please delete the previous paragraph]

As I was about to reach into my pocket for my phone, something caught my ear.

Ouija.

Laughter erupted from the men next to me, causing everybody in the pub to look in my direction. I hunched over the table, hoping no one would see me.

For a second I thought I'd imagined hearing it. I'd done a lot of research into 'talking' or 'spirit' boards years ago, none of which made it into any of my novels. I didn't think my readers would be convinced by a haunted board, especially after the onslaught of Hollywood movies that exploited them for cheap scares. Unlike in those films, in reality the board didn't burst into flames or rocket across the room like a flying saucer. Besides, few boards were supposedly haunted or cursed anyway, and existed simply to communicate with a spirit, or spirits, good or bad. Though I'd once really wanted to believe in it, especially after my parent's passing, I'd decided none of it was true. It was easier to move on from the grief that way, or at least ignore it. Being teased with the possibility of contacting them would have been too tempting.

There was also the scientific explanation: the 'ideomotor effect', tiny movements one makes unconsciously. It was a theory I'd subscribed to, but it wasn't the reason I dropped the idea: I could exploit any object for added mystery or for a plot device. I just feared my readers would have Ouija fatigue.

Maybe my hearing of the word was my subconscious telling me to read up on it again, a prompt to start writing. But it was the funny pronunciation that made me doubt that, for I hadn't heard "Ouija" exactly, but "*wee-jee*."

The men at the table had fallen quiet. I wondered if I'd heard it from them. I glanced in their direction. Two had their backs to me. It looked like they were playing a card game; I couldn't quite see with the brim of my cap restricting my view. Just as I raised it, an older man at the table, possibly in his seventies, looked up and caught my gaze. His green eyes flashed.

A large glass banged down hard on the table beside me, making me jump.

"Your water, sir," the bartender said. "Sorry, didn't mean to scare ya.'"

"He's away with the fairies, Bertha," the old man growled.

"G'way with your nonsense," the bartender snapped, rolling her eyes before heading back to the bar.

I didn't dare look up again, afraid the old man might call me over; I wasn't in the mood to talk. *He might have known my parents,* I suddenly realised. Everyone knew everyone around here. *And then all the weddings and funerals. He might recognise me from one of them, even in my haggard state.*

Then doubt crept in. Why had Rachel chosen my home county for a break? Surely it would only stir up old memories, as well as those more recent. My parents, their funerals, leaving them to rest in peace, never to return to that quiet corner in the graveyard.

"Your stew, sir," the bartender announced, placing a massive bowl on the table. The stew was thick and creamy-looking, with fat chunks of vegetables. *Hearty,* I thought.

"Anything else?" she asked.

"No thanks, all good."

My stomach growled angrily, and the feelings of doubt quickly subsided. I wolfed down the stew, despite it being piping hot. My tongue burned instantly, but I was too hungry to care. When I finished it, I gulped the glass of water.

"Thirsty?"

I glanced at the table beside me and put down my empty glass. The old man was staring directly at me.

Why was he watching *me*?

I nodded, resting my chin in my palm to cover one side of my face.

"You travelled far?"

He mustn't know me, then. Perhaps he was trying to be friendly, though his comment earlier about me being dazed was a bit odd.

"Yes, I suppose," I answered. "I've just come from London."

"Jaysus." He scratched the stubble on his cheek. "Queer place to come to from London."

"It's not too bad," I said. The two younger men turned around now. *Don't tell them everything,* I told myself. They were all looking at me, waiting for me to continue talking. The silence was making me uncomfortable. "I like it," I continued, trying hard to hold my tongue. "I think."

"I bet you think we're all backward," he said, curtly. "Bertha, get this man another drink."

"No, no, it's alright," I said, trying desperately to think of an excuse to get up and leave. I'd had my dinner now; there was no reason for me to stay.

"Don't be silly!" he barked, pulling an empty chair towards him. Its legs grated against the tiled floor, causing heads to turn. *They'll all see you now,* was all I could think. *See how ugly you look...*

"C'mon," he said, bundling the cards together. "We were just about to play a game."

I knew I had to get up – there was no refusing Irish hospitality – but doing so would mean everyone would see me. They'd see my face, even with the cap. *But will they recognise me?* I wondered. This man didn't seem to. And wasn't I older now, and uglier?

The heat from the fire made me sweat, my T-shirt beginning to stick to my back. I regretted leaving my scarf on. I kept my head down, my eyes fixed on the empty chair.

"What are ya' drinking?" the old man asked as I settled awkwardly into the chair.

"Just water," I replied. I gripped the edge of the chair to stop my hands shaking. I was very, very close to getting up and running back to the cottage. It'd been a long time since I sat down at a table with anyone other than Rachel. My heart beat wildly, my whole body clammy. I wasn't ready for this. And my body knew it.

"Water?" the old man jeered. There were sniggers from the other two men. "You must be joking? You can't come into an Irish pub and drink water!"

"I'm fine, really," I stated. Sweat was gathering on the nape of my neck. I was too close to the fire. I had to get away. I had to get out.

"It'll be on the house," the man assured me.

I simply smiled, but inside my heart was hammering, growing louder in my ears. "But just a half pint," I blurted. "I've got to drive."

"That's the spirit," the old man said, clasping my shoulder as he got to his feet. I watched his muddy boots disappear as he made his way to the bar.

"Nice gloves," one of the men commented. I was still wearing them – a habit of mine at this time of the year – so I wedged both hands between my thighs. *What else are they looking at?* I wondered.

A long silence followed.

"Into card games?" the man to my left finally asked.

"No," I answered, unable to raise my eyes to meet his.

"Good," he said. "I can't stand another game."

"Ah, he's only trying," the man on my right said. "He's mad for these aul games nights. God knows we need a bit more community around here. It's grim enough."

"I don't think it's grim," I interjected, looking up.

Both men appeared younger than me, no more than thirty, with rosy cheeks and youthful complexions. *All the fresh air,* I thought. They wore thick woollen jumpers with holes and dirty jeans, though the man on my left wore glasses. He was tall and lean with narrow shoulders, whereas the younger man on my right was short, broad and bulky, possibly a gym-goer, or just a very strong farmer. I wondered if they were brothers.

"It's a nice change to London," I added. "The lake I'm staying near is beautiful."

"The lake?" the younger man asked, before they both exchanged a glance.

A pint glass landed on the table in front of me, filled with a reddish-brown liquid.

"What happened to the half pint?" I asked.

"They ran out," the old man quipped. He planted his arm on my shoulder as he sat down. Then, taking a sip of his own pint, he looked directly at me with his bright green eyes. His nose was round, red and inflamed as though he had the flu, though more likely it was from drinking too much whiskey. White, prickly stubble peppered his rosy, wrinkled cheeks. His clothes were worn, his trousers and shoes muddy. I suspected he was a local farmer.

"I know you," he said, studying my face.

Immediately, I sipped my pint, hoping this would conceal my face. It tasted bitter, like ale.

He put his drink down and leant over, his eyes narrowing. An overpowering mixture of alcohol and cigarette smoke took me back to being a child squeezed between drunks in the back seat of the car that my parents had picked up, all on their way to the next pub.

The man leant closer, raising a finger. "You're Mulrooney's son, aren't you?"

I almost spat the drink back into the glass.

There's no leaving now.

He sat back, furrowing his wild, bushy brows. I wasn't sure if it was because we'd stopped talking, but suddenly the whole pub seemed to have become silent.

I nodded and put down my drink. "Yes."

"Oh." His eyes widened, as if he'd said something wrong. "I'm sorry about your loss, erm…"

"Rick," I offered. "And it's okay. I've moved past that now. Well, if only my writing had moved on too."

"You're the writer – yes!" he gasped, his eyes growing even bigger. "Rick Rooney. I saw you in the paper years ago. Ah, so you're back from the big smoke then?"

I nodded, cringing at the use of the truncated name, Rooney – a name my marketing team had bestowed upon me. "Mulrooney will simply never shift a million copies," my editor, Pierce, had explained.

"Jesus," the shorter man said. "Never thought I'd meet a celebrity."

"I'm not a celebrity," I said quickly. "More a declining

mid-list author." The young men gawked at me. I probably shouldn't use industry jargon around here. "I mean, most authors are like me," I continued. "Just trying to get by. The pay isn't what it used to be. In fact, I rely mostly on my partner."

"Be God," the old man said, extending his hand. The rough skin grated against mine. "I'm Mick, Mick Flanagan. You wouldn't know me, but your father would've. And these are my nephews, Tom and Adam."

"What was that idea you had earlier, Uncle?" the younger brother, Adam, asked. "About the weejee board?"

"Shut up," his brother snapped.

"Would you play the weejee?" Mick asked me.

Tom folded his arms and rolled his eyes. It was clear he didn't want to play, for whatever reason.

"I don't know," I answered, thinking of an excuse to leave.

"Sure, don't you write the horror?" Adam asked. "I thought you'd be into all that."

"Yes, I do," I said. "But that doesn't mean I have to believe it. It's just what I choose to write. It pays the bills anyway."

Or at least, paid...

"Aye, well now's your chance," Mick said, rubbing his hands together excitedly. "First-hand experience. You can't get better than that. You could even write a book about it."

"We could all be in it," Adam shouted, causing a few heads to turn.

"Adam!" his uncle snapped. "You're not at home, have some cop-on."

Maybe Adam was a lot younger than I'd thought, possibly late teens.

"Bertha," Mick called, waving a hand.

"No, Uncle," Tom said, his eyes widening.

I glanced behind me to see the bartender appear behind the counter. "What are ye' asking for now?" she bellowed.

"Bertha, can you bring out that aul board?" Mick asked.

"Which board? We've got loads of feckin' boards around here."

"You know the one," Mick said.

She froze, momentarily, before clearing her throat. "We don't play that out here. You know that, Mick. It could – you know..." She leant over the table to whisper, "Scare the other customers."

"Fine," Mick said. He got to his feet. "We'll move into the back, then."

"Uncle," Tom began, putting a hand on his Mick's arm. "The card games are fine."

"Ah, stop," Mick said, throwing away Tom's hand. "We used to have some great craic with the aul weejee."

"That was fifty years ago, Mick," Bertha remarked. "No one wants to play that anymore."

"I'm hardly that old, Bertha. Are *ye* comin'?" Mick beckoned, getting to his feet.

I looked at the two brothers, shrugging my shoulders.

"I dunno," Tom said, rubbing his arm nervously. "Wouldn't it be dangerous, like, it being Halloween and all?"

"What's dangerous about a board?" Mick asked.

"I mean, I don't really believe in it, so it doesn't matter to me," I offered as the two brothers were silent. At this point, I'd accepted I wasn't leaving anytime soon, so I might as well offer my insight. "I've never had anything supernatural happen," I added. Tom shuffled in his chair, seeming far from convinced. "And if it is true, I know how to play," I continued. "Properly, I mean. The right way."

I think I also wanted to prove to myself it was a load of nonsense, that there was nothing remotely scary about these boards, and that it wasn't worth writing about.

"That's sorted, then," Mick said, picking up his drink. "We've got the expert author here. Bertha, show us to the board."

In a Corner of a Dark Room

Bertha showed us through some curtains and into a dimly lit backroom, muttering under her breath. The lights on the wall flickered, and an old, damp smell permeated the air, as if the room had been left unused for some time. We placed our drinks on a round table in the corner.

"It's on the shelf there," Bertha pointed above the table. "I'd rather not touch the thing."

"So you're a believer, then?" Adam asked. Bertha didn't answer. We watched Mick retrieve the largest box and set it down on the table, wiping dust from the surface. His hands hovered over the rectangular box before he removed the lid. His eyes glinted.

"Can I get ye anything else to drink?" Bertha finally said.

"Same again," Mick announced, removing the lid of the box.

"Right ye are," she sighed, then disappeared through the curtain.

"I'm not sure about this," Tom said, watching Mick lift the board from the box and plant it in the middle of the table.

"Yer a bunch of sissies," Mick spat. He cast the box aside and sat in front of it, rubbing his hands together, Adam taking a seat next to him. "I watched people play this many a time and nothin' spooky ever happened."

"So what's the point, then?" Tom asked.

"That's a misconception about spirit boards," I interjected. "People assume only spooky things happen when, in reality, it's really quite mundane."

"In reality?" Tom asked. I noticed his bottom lip tremble.

"I mean, those who claim to have experienced something have only received mundane messages, like hello or goodbye, or they felt a presence – nothing more than that. Certainly nothing evil."

I could see I wasn't making Tom any more comfortable. He scratched his head doubtfully.

"Look, it was all their doing anyway," I said. "The messages. And what they felt. It was all in their head." I didn't bother going into the ideomotor effect; it would take too long to explain.

I dropped my cap and jacket on a vacant chair and turned my attention to the board. It looked old, older than any spirit boards I'd seen up close. There was no branding of the product name 'Ouija' on the board either – it was just a regular spirit board. Although they weren't technically wrong: 'We-ja', 'Wee-Ja' and even 'Weed-ja' were some other names in circulation for these boards. I leaned in for a closer look. Letters of the alphabet were painted in a curve along the top with the numbers 1 to 9 and 0 in a straight line below. Above the letters were the words *Yes* and *No* and below the numbers *Goodbye*. Each corner had a symbol: a full moon in the top-left corner, a half-moon in the top-right, a star in the bottom left and, oddly, a swastika in the bottom-right.

"How old is this?" I asked, taking a seat.

Mick shrugged. "I dunno, but I'd say it's been here at this pub for a hundred years. My father used to play it, as well as his father."

"Weirdness runs in the family, then," Tom remarked. He took his seat slowly and very close to me, most likely for comfort.

I examined the board again. "It looks like it's from the 1920s. Or even older." I glanced up at Mick. "When did you say you played with it?"

"Oh, decades ago," he said. "These young ones would prefer to play on their phones now."

"At least the dead can't reach us through our phones," Tom said quickly, a quiver in his voice.

"I'd say those phones are more dangerous," Mick countered. "You're all acting like addicts."

"Some spirit board players are addicts," I said, sipping my drink. All three men looked at me. "I mean, some people form an attachment, end up placing all their trust in these things."

"Look, are we going to play this thing or not?" Adam asked.

Mick cleared his throat and laid the planchette in the middle of the board. It was large and triangular, the size of a small plate, with a round hole, or window, in the middle to see the letters and numbers. "Come on," he ordered, gesturing for us to rest our fingers on the pointer too.

"This is ridiculous," Tom said, though he leant over nonetheless. His breathing was heavy and his fingers were damp when he placed them next to mine.

Mick closed his eyes. I closed mine too, and waited for him to speak. After a few seconds of silence, I opened them.

"Aren't you going to call someone?" I asked.

Mick opened an eye. "Call someone?"

"Yes," I sighed. "Haven't you played before?"

"We used to let the pointer move itself."

"That's dangerous," I said. "That's not how you should play."

Tom looked at me quizzically. "We need to call on someone specific, not let any old spirit in."

"Fine," Mick said. "And who would you suggest?"

"I don't know any dead people," Adam said, sitting back.

I knew that couldn't be true. I took a sip of ale, thinking.

"Fine," I said finally. "I'll do it."

"Should we light a candle?" Adam asked.

"No need. They're mostly lit for atmosphere. We just need to be able to see the board. Now, two things," I said, remembering my research. "Stay calm throughout. I don't want any of you losing it at the slightest, mundane movement. It could just be one of us moving the planchette without realising. But if spirits actually exist, apparently they can sense fear, and some may take advantage of that." I felt Tom's fingers trembling. "Just stay calm. And stay in control. Otherwise we'll only freak ourselves out. Finally," I continued, "we must end the session properly. No running away or packing up the board. We must instruct them to leave first. Let them say goodbye. Then we can leave."

"*Them*?" Tom asked.

"Spirits," I said. "But it's highly doubtful, Tom. And don't ask too difficult questions."

"Not even about the lottery?" Adam asked.

"No," I said. "If spirits do exist, then they only know as much as we know, unless we call on someone who was psychic. Just simple questions, okay?"

"This is nonsense," Tom remarked.

"I'd much rather we were in the right frame of mind before diving into it," I said.

"Hurry up!" Mick snapped, his leg trembling beside me, presumably out of agitation.

"Okay." I took a deep breath. "First, everyone close their eyes and imagine a circle around us. This circle is our protection from any unwanted spirits. Do not leave and break the circle. Breaking the circle is their invitation."

I peeped out of one eye. To my surprise, everyone had closed their eyes. "Good," I said. "Now – we wish to communicate with the spirits of Patrick and Jane Mulrooney."

Silence fell. I think we were all holding our breaths, waiting. All I heard was the murmur of voices from the bar.

Then something squeaked behind me. I sensed Tom jump in his chair. I turned to see Bertha standing before the curtain, a tray of drinks in her hands. "I'll just leave this here," she said quickly, placing the tray on a table before darting from the room.

Adam sighed. "Shit." Sweat gleamed on his forehead.

Mick shuffled, rising to his feet. "Don't!" I started. "Remember, we mustn't break the circle. We can have those drinks after." He sat back down, not without a roll of his eyes. I closed mine again, hoping the circle was still intact.

"We wish to speak to Patrick and Jane Mulrooney," I announced. I focused on my fingers. Would the planchette move? Could my parents *really* be contacted? "If Patrick or Jane Mulrooney are with us, speak to us through the board."

I was just about to open my mouth to speak when my legs tingled. I didn't think much of it, assuming I was becoming increasingly aware and sensitive and just tuning in to a part of my body. But the tingling moved up through my knees, through my thighs, making my legs jump. My knees banged against the table.

"Woah!" Adam exclaimed.

"Sorry," I said, keeping my eyes closed. "That was just me.

Must be the cold."

"It *has* gone cold," Tom commented.

"Would ye ever be quiet?" Mick muttered. I hadn't expected him to be so involved. Then again, he was the one who had wanted to play. He must have believed it, even partially.

"If you are present," I said, "please use the board to—"

The planchette moved. I wasn't sure who was moving it, but I guessed it was Tom, as at the same moment I sensed him shivering. I opened my eyes to see the planchette had moved to the top of the board, directly above the word *Hello*.

"Christ!" Adam gasped, his eyes wide.

"That wasn't me," I said, looking around.

Tom and Mick opened their eyes too.

Mick shrugged. "Wasn't me."

"Nor me," Tom said, pushing up his glasses.

If it wasn't any of them, then who could it be? It could hardly be my parents.

Could it?

"Go on," Mick pressed. "Ask something."

"If someone is with us, please spell out your name."

We all watched in silence, holding our breaths. Tom's finger was shaking visibly now, and I wondered if he had unknowingly caused the movement. A cold breeze touched the nape of my neck, making my whole body shudder. I stared at our fingers, forgetting about the cold, watching closely for the slightest movement. In the corner of my eye, I thought I saw the lights flicker, but I kept my gaze fixed.

Then something remarkable happened. The planchette began to move. I felt no push from Mick or his nephews. Instead, it seemed to glide by itself, taking us along. *Impossible,* I thought.

"J," Mick said, reading the letter over which the planchette had stopped. Then it moved very slowly to the left. "I."

"What's it saying?" Adam asked.

"I don't know," I replied, still unable to comprehend it had actually moved.

The planchette moved again, this time to the right of the board, almost to the edge.

"M," Mick noted.

I looked up. The colour had drained from Adam's face, the once rosy cheeks now shadowed grey.

"Jim?" I asked. "Who's Jim?"

No one answered, their eyes fixed on the board. I didn't know any Jim. Certainly no one in my family was called Jim.

Where are my parents? Why haven't they come?

"I don't like this," Adam said abruptly, squirming.

"We can't leave," I reminded him. "Not until he's said goodbye."

I was glad, then, that we'd been following the rules. Or at least, I thought we still were.

Suddenly the planchette swerved to the centre of the board, hovering over the letter H.

"No!" Adam shouted. His eyes were wide, his mouth hanging open. His cheeks were no longer red. Mick was also pale and unmoving.

"We mustn't stop," I reminded them.

"We have to," Adam insisted.

"Be quiet, Adam," Tom said, shushing him. "It was just stories."

"What stories?" I asked.

The planchette moved again, all the way to the other side of the board, all the way to A. I realised Mick had stopped announcing the letters. The planchette moved down the board, stopping at R.

"Jim Har," I read.

"Don't!" Adam warned.

"What's wrong?" I asked.

"The board is fucking alive, that's what's wrong!" Tom shouted.

"Be quiet, lads," Mick whispered.

I peered down at the board. The planchette was still fixed over R. Then it moved to the left, stopping at O.

"It can't be," Mick muttered slowly, astonished.

"What is it?" I looked up at him. What was it they weren't telling me? Who was this person?

Then my arm was suddenly swung towards the letter W.

That was his name, then.

"Jim Harrow," I whispered.

A bang sounded from beyond the curtains, like something exploding. Someone screamed, then shouts came from the main bar.

Adam jumped to his feet.

"Adam!" I shouted.

But he didn't respond. He swung around, his hand knocking his pint glass as he ran. The glass wobbled before tipping off the edge of the table, smashing on the floor.

"Adam, come back!" I called.

Now Mick and Tom were both on their feet as well, their faces white.

"That's enough of that," Mick said, pulling a cap from his pocket.

"Mick, we have to close the session."

He laughed nervously, before planting a cap on his head. "I'll leave you, the expert, to do that."

I looked at Tom. His glasses had almost slid off his nose. "I'm going with him," he announced. "I've had enough too."

"What happened?" Bertha's head poked through the curtains, her eyes scanning the room before finding the smashed glass. "I want ye out of here," she ordered. "And put away that flippin' board."

Mick and Tom threw on their coats, rushing past Bertha without a word.

"Put it away!" she barked, before disappearing through the curtain.

The planchette still sat over the letter W. Should I close the session? Was it too late, if all of this was indeed real? The protective circle, if one had existed, was surely gone now, along with Mick and his nephews.

I retrieved the box. As much as I wanted to put the board away, I still wondered if there was anything I could do to close the session correctly.

I whispered, "Leave us."

Nothing stirred. Not even the light flickered.

"Leave us now," I ordered.

I held the box tight, staring at the board, waiting for the planchette to move. If this Jim Harrow had heard me, then the planchette should move to *Goodbye*. If he had said "Hello," then surely this too was possible? But what if he had already gone? What if we had scared him away?

"What are you playing at?" I heard myself say aloud. I stepped away from the board, clocking that I might have been tricked. "You idiot," I muttered as I put the board back in the box. "You've been played."

Of course that's what happened, I thought. *They were only messing with me. I bet that's what they always do to newcomers to this pub.*

And that explains the loud bang? And the screams? Maybe it was just coincidence. Someone must have smashed their glass. It's a pub, after all. Glasses smash.

I placed the box back on the shelf, before downing the rest of my pint, hoping that would quell these thoughts.

△

"Had enough, have ya?" Bertha asked as I approached the counter, leaving the other four pints untouched.

The pub had almost entirely emptied, except for a couple of men still drinking at the bar.

I pulled my cap down, feeling embarrassed. Ashamed, even though I was the one who'd fallen victim to their prank.

"I'd like to pay now," I said, reaching inside my jacket pocket.

"I'm sure you would," she replied scornfully. "It's 47 euros for the lot of ye."

"They didn't pay?"

"Ha!" someone yelped from the other side of bar, near the door. One of the last of the drinkers. "You should have seen their faces," he said. "White as ghosts they were."

I looked at Bertha again. "I thought they'd be used to this by now."

"Used to it?" Bertha asked, her brows knitting.

"I bet this is what they do to all newcomers like me?"

Bertha stared at me, hard. Then she leant on the countertop. "Young man, if that was true, I'd have gotten rid of it long ago. And I won't be taking it out again any time soon. Feckin' weejee. Don't know why we've held onto the thing for so long."

"But they were just playing with me. A Halloween trick or something."

"And that explains the light, does it?" She nodded at a light bulb on the wall. It had blown to pieces, leaving a dark stain on the yellow wallpaper. *The loud bang.* Pieces of glass were scattered across an empty table and chairs. "The couple there had to leave because of ye."

"I'm so sorry. I'm happy to cover the bulb."

"No," she said firmly. "You can cover those fellas' drinks. Mick and themselves."

"Of course." I handed her my credit card.

She shook her head. "We only take cash here."

I was a little surprised, having been so long since I'd actually used cash. In London, almost everything is contactless. Luckily, I'd taken out some notes at Heathrow. I dug into my wallet, then handed over a fifty.

"You can keep the change," I said.

She snapped the note from me. "Good night, Mister…"

"Mulrooney."

"Ah, of course," she mused, squinting as if examining my face. I wondered if she'd known my parents. But I was far too tired to bring it up.

"Good night, and sorry again," I said.

"That's alright. Take care of yourself, Mister Mulrooney."

I smiled and nodded. Just as I was about to turn, I remembered the name from the board. I hadn't had the chance to ask Mick or his nephews. "You haven't heard of a Jim Harrow, have you?" I asked.

She stared at me momentarily, her eyes locked with mine. Her lips moved, very slightly. "I think it'd be best if you left now, Mister Mulrooney," she said.

“Sure.” I took a step backwards. “No worries.”

“And I don’t want to see you here again.”

The Way Back

It was the first time I'd ever been barred from anywhere. Sure, I'd been a little rebellious as a teenager, like any teen – or at least I pretended to be – but I'd never actually been barred from an establishment. It was odd. Why was I being blamed for what happened? Wasn't it Mick's idea after all?

I hurried down the road, shining my phone light in front of me, wanting nothing more than to be back at the cottage. I couldn't help shake the awkwardness, the embarrassment, even shame. I didn't expect to be excommunicated on my first night home.

My heart was pounding, and I didn't know whether it was from the adrenaline of playing with the spirit board or from being barred, or both. But the name had clearly upset Adam, and the others. Could that really have been pretence? If so, it was the best acting I'd ever seen. And if they were just playing with me, why choose a name I wouldn't know? Was I expected to know? Was Jim Harrow some local mythical figure that drew tourists here that I somehow didn't know about?

As I hurried back to the bridge, I tried to think of all the names and stories I'd heard while growing up. I remembered the usual characters, like the pooka, the banshee, the fairy, but nothing related to a Jim Harrow.

My heart was still pounding in my ears, so loud I could barely hear my footsteps. I realised I couldn't see very far in front of me; the bridge was nowhere in sight. When I pointed my phone downwards, I couldn't even see my own hands. In fact, I couldn't see a thing. I stopped and turned around, expecting to see the lights from the pub, but there was only darkness.

A thick fog had descended, blocking the pub lights, the stars and the moon. I was so wrapped up in my own thoughts, I hadn't even registered it. It must have been gathering all evening, and I'd somehow stumbled into the thick of it.

I studied the fog closely, suddenly aware of the cold dampness that stuck to my face like a sticky cobweb. My nose tickled. I tried to pull at it, but the wet sheet still clung to my skin. I was used to fog or, more specifically, smog, in London, but it had never stuck to me like this. I was surrounded by the stuff. I wanted to run as fast I could, back to the safety of the cottage. Only I didn't know the way.

I felt around for the edge of the road with my shoes. Wet grass brushed against my ankles. Hoping this was the roadside, I continued the same way I had been going, desperate to locate the bridge. At least then I'd know where I was. I broke into a jog, keeping to the side of the road, my shoes thumping on thick grass, desperate to return to the cottage.

Minutes later, I thought I heard a faint trickling sound. I hurried onwards, hoping it was the river under the bridge. My face was covered in a mixture of cold sweat and damp. I wiped it with my sleeve, before dabbing the sweat gathering on my forehead. It was then I realised I couldn't hear any water.

Had I crossed it already?

I paused, listening closely, but hearing only the loud thudding of my heart. Puzzled, I stood motionless, hoping my heart would slow down so I could hear properly. No other sound came. I shone the light, hoping the bridge might materialise. There was only fog, and strings of shimmering webs floating past my phone, sticking to my eyelashes and brows.

I walked backwards, hoping to return to the water, almost stumbling over clumps of grass and fallen branches. And still, I heard no trickling sound. I was astonished. How could the river disappear? I'd heard it only minutes ago. Had the fog somehow blocked out the sound too? I must have forgotten what thick, country fog was like.

Shivering from the cold, and feeling increasingly vulnerable, I walked ahead again, keeping to the ditch, determined to stay on route.

It was then that I heard another sound. A sharp clip-clap, like footsteps, in addition to my own. I stopped, ears pricked. The footsteps stopped too. I guessed I'd just heard my own echo. I started walking again and heard the footsteps, milliseconds behind my own. As I walked faster, so too did the other footsteps, the sounds growing even louder, a harder clip-clap.

Was it my own echo? Was the fog playing tricks with sound? Either way, I broke into a sprint, running faster than I'd run in years. The footsteps only grew louder and closer. Who was it? Mick and his nephews trying to scare me again?

"Go away!" I found myself shouting, hoping to scare whoever it was away. Strangely, I heard no echo, only the sounds of footsteps.

Coming closer.

Clip-clap.

Someone was behind me, and they were about to catch up.

I might have frozen in fear, but instead my legs gathered momentum, and I focused only on reaching the cottage as quickly as possible. I continued sprinting, shining the light ahead of me, desperate to catch sight of a forest tree, where the narrow path back to the cottage would be. But I still couldn't see anything except the fog. My body shook violently. I fought the urge to simply collapse, focusing instead on the phone light ahead of me, and trying to block out the growing sound of the footsteps.

Clip-clap. Clip-clap. Clip-clap.

I had to reach the forest soon, surely? Where else could I be? It must be just around the…

A tap on my left shoulder made me gasp. I swung around, with only my phone to hit back, and saw a severely scarred hand reach out from the fog, its fingers sharp claws. I yelped, falling backwards. The hand withdrew, disappearing back into the fog. As I crashed onto my back, two great lights, like eyes, appeared in the dark. The lights were blinding, forcing my eyes closed. A loud horn sounded, and then I heard a rush of wind that knocked me into the wet ditch. I continued to fall, further and further, until I couldn't hear anything at all.

Jim Harrow

My mouth was uncomfortably dry. I reached out, hoping to locate a glass of water. I usually leave something on my bedside table the night before, although not always water. Mostly sleep medication or alcohol, whichever I need that night.

I heard footsteps beside me.

Clip-clap.

Clip-clap.

"No," I moaned, swinging my arms, too scared to open my eyes. What if I saw that scarred and withered hand reaching for me through the fog, the long claws wrapping around my arm, seizing me?

"No!" I shouted.

"It's okay."

It was a deep voice – not Rachel's. I wanted Rachel. I missed her. Why had I left her? She was the only one who could wake me from this horrible nightmare.

"Rachel?" I cried. "Rachel, please!"

"Ssh, ssh." It was a man's voice. A soft hand pressed against my forehead, then rubbed my cheek. "Drink this," he instructed, and then I felt cold glass press against my dry lips. The liquid was strong, alcoholic, reminding me of the pub. Then I remembered Mick, Adam and Tom and the spirit board. The name it had spelt.

Jim Harrow.

"Jim!" I shouted, opening my eyes.

The man crouched beside me, pushing a glass to my lips.

"Drink!" he instructed. "It will help."

I leant forward and sipped. The liquid burnt my throat as I swallowed it. I winced, pushing the glass away.

"It's good brandy," the man said. "It's been sitting here a long time."

"I don't need any more drink," I mumbled. I pressed a hand to my head. There was a dull throbbing there, and I wasn't sure if I'd been hit or if it was the onset of a hangover. I tried to move my neck to look at the man, but a pain shot from my neck to my head; it was incredibly stiff.

"Glad to see you're alive," the man said, standing up. "You're not the first I've seen passed out on that road."

I tried to sit up instead to take in this stranger. He had his back to the fireplace in the cottage hearth. He was well-dressed, I observed, not like Mick and his nephews, wearing a tweed jacket, a purple jumper and a striped tie. He had a long, straight nose and a clean-shaven, strong jaw, even though his face was a little plump. Only his grey hair aged him. Greyer than mine, but tidily combed.

"Who are you?" I asked, pressing a hand to my aching neck.

"Brian," he smiled, the skin creasing around his dark brown eyes. "I only wanted to drop by and see if everything was alright. I didn't expect to find my guest passed out in a ditch."

"Shit," I whispered. "Sorry! I wasn't drunk. Well, maybe partially."

"I'm sure," Brian said, retrieving a stool from the kitchen. He positioned it by the hearth and sat down, his back to the fire.

He folded his arms and looked me up and down. He'd taken on the look of a schoolteacher, waiting for a student to confess to something naughty. His large, inquisitive eyes made me anxious. I looked around for my cap.

"What are you looking for?" he asked.

"My cap," I answered.

"I didn't see any cap. I did find a phone, though it looks badly damaged." He slipped his hand inside his jacket pocket and held out my phone. "Did you get hit or something?"

"No," I replied, taking the phone. The screen was completely cracked, reducing most visibility, but the backlight was still working. I'd have to get the screen replaced. I placed the phone on the small coffee table beside me. "I don't think so," I continued, remembering the headlights and the horn. "I think they just swerved past. It felt close, though. I must have looked like a right wreck, lying in a ditch."

"As I've said, I've seen others." He tightened his arms around himself as if he was cold.

"There was someone there," I recalled. "I think they followed me from the pub. I could hear their footsteps and then…" I winced. "And then this… this hand reached out and tried to grab me."

"A hand?" he exclaimed. "Did you see who it was?"

I considered this. "No," I said, and reached for the glass of brandy.

"Here, let me fill that up." Brian slipped from the stool and headed to the kitchen, returning with a half-empty bottle. "Sorry," he said as he topped up my glass. "I had some myself. You've been sleeping for hours." He picked up another glass from the coffee table. "Do you mind?"

"No, of course not," I said. "What time is it?"

"Four in the morning."

"Shit! Sorry—"

"It's okay," Brian smiled. "How much did you drink?"

"Not much," I replied. "Honestly. A couple of pints, I think."

"Right," he said dubiously. "So you're saying someone jumped out at you and, what, gave you an awful fright?"

"I think so." How did I pass out exactly? From fright? Shock? "We were playing a game," I recalled. "These locals made me play with a spirit board. I think they were trying to scare me. I think they followed me from the pub."

I looked up to find him staring into his drink. "Let me guess," he began, swirling his brandy. "They summoned the spirit of Jim Harrow?"

"Yes." I nodded and tried to sit up fully. It was only then I realised I was lying under a raincoat. "How did you know?"

He smiled before taking a swig of his drink. "It's always Jim Harrow around here. I just wished they'd leave that man alone."

"Who is he?"

"Jim Harrow was the owner of the Harrow Inn. Castlestrange Lodge to you. Many years ago, long before I was born. I'd heard my father talk about the Harrow Inn. It was simply the Harrow, back then. That was before the fire in 1939. That's why they changed the name."

"The fire?" I asked.

"I'm rambling now," he said. He topped up our glasses. "In the thirties, a travelling guest left your spirit board in a room at the Harrow. They were very popular back then. I personally prefer to stay well clear of anything occult. I mean, I had to..." He paused and cleared his throat. "But it was just a popular game then. And Jim Harrow was interested in this board. Soon it became more than a game for Jim. He started bringing the board out almost every night. He became transfixed. The more he'd played, the more he'd drink. And when he was drunk, all he wanted to do was play with the board."

"It became an addiction," I commented.

"Yes." Brian gazed into his glass.

I remembered from my research how some users became dependent on the board once it was incorporated into their daily lives. They'd use the board for every question imaginable. Every decision. They'd given too much power to the board, and it started to control them.

"One night," Brian continued, "long after the pub had closed, so the story goes, Jim kept playing with the board. He'd been drinking the inn into debt, and his house was soon to be repossessed. Jim asked the board what he should do. And the board said it needed a sacrifice to save the pub. It needed Jim's family. So Jim left the pub, taking all the bottles he could carry, and headed home." He paused, his eyes staring above me. "Then he set the house alight as his family slept, burning them alive." He took a large mouthful of his drink.

I was too stunned to respond. What if it was true? What if it really was Jim Harrow we'd contacted through the board? What if it was his burnt hand I'd seen, coming for me?

"There are other versions of the story however," Brian continued. "Some sources say he lit the fire to save his son, who was sick at the time. The board instructed him to light a fire around his son's bed to cast the malady out. It's not clear, and you know how stories change over time."

"What happened to Jim?" I asked. "Did he die?"

"Eventually, but not with his family. Some of the locals had spotted the fire and ran to the house. They'd heard screaming and shouting. They knew it was Jim. He emerged from the front door in flames, begging for forgiveness, apparently, before running down the field and throwing himself in the lake."

"This lake?" I asked, nodding to the window.

Brian shook his head and placed his empty glass on the table.

"That explains why Tom asked," I said. Seeing Brian's confusion, I clarified, "When I said I was staying at the lake, one of the locals I played with seemed surprised. Now I realise he was scared."

"That explains it, then," Brian exclaimed, clasping his knees. "You planted the idea in their head."

"No, not Tom's. He seemed reluctant. But the others were eager to play. That's where they must have got the Jim Harrow idea. Still, it doesn't make the story any less disturbing, especially since it happened so close to here."

"And that's what it is, Rick. It's just a story. There was no evidence Jim threw himself into the lake. For all we know, he burnt with his family in the house."

"You mean they never found his body?" I asked.

"If you call ash and dust his body." He looked into my eyes and smiled. "I think you've had enough scares for one night. I'm sure it was those locals playing games. What were their names again?"

"Mick, Tom and Adam."

"I suggest you stay away from them, and maybe Castlestrange Lodge too."

"That's easy," I said. Then I added, "I've been barred."

"Hmm. Perhaps for the best." Brian stood up straight. "I'll let you sleep. I'll bring more of that if you like." He nodded at the brandy bottle. "I feel bad for drinking most of it."

"Don't. You've done enough."

He nodded, then retrieved his hat from a hook on the cottage door. "Good night, Mister Mulrooney." He smiled and opened the door, letting in a cold draft that made me shiver.

"Good night," I said. "And thanks again. For helping me."

"No problem." He nodded, securing his hat. "If there's anything else I can do, give me a shout. You have my number."

"Will do. Good night."

Though he closed the door behind him, he left a chill in the air. I got up to move closer to the fire, which was now reduced to embers. Brian had given me enough information to start drafting a novel. But I wasn't interested in novelising the Jim Harrow story then; it was too frightening. I didn't like how the story had ended in the lake just across from the cottage.

I stared into the dying embers, unable to banish that ravaged hand from my head. Had I imagined it? Or was it Mick or Adam, conjuring one last scare? But it had been scarred, the flesh withered like it had been burnt. Would they really have gone to all that effort, especially when I'd no clue who Jim Harrow was? And the way they'd run from the back bar looked genuine. Adam had knocked his glass over, and Mick and Tom had followed him without even saying goodbye. Perhaps only one of them had been playing a trick. Maybe it was Mick's sick joke. The highlight of games night.

My eyelids were heavy, the brandy having made me drowsy. I lay back on the couch, pulling the dry raincoat over me. *It must be Brian's*, I thought. Why had he been so kind? Perhaps he knew me. Everyone around here seemed to know my parents.

I decided I'd sleep there, under the raincoat, as I was too tired and achy to get undressed and move to the bedroom. I gazed into the dying embers, hoping sleep would come soon, and the worst of my stay at Black Lake was behind me.

III

Anne, 1939

Letter from Anne Harrow to Maud Kavanagh

Fairy Hill
18th March 1939

Dear Maud,

Bless you for your last letter. Sorry it has taken me ages to write back to you – I've had my hands full with the little one.

It looks like the winter is behind us at long last. It snowed again before wee Brendan went back to school, and I know it was the chill that got him this time. Poor child was in bed all week. Your brother insisted we give him a drop of poteen, but I just cannot bear the thought of giving that lethal drink to a child, especially someone as poorly as Brendan. It may have worked on you and your brother back in the day, but I'm sure there are better remedies out there now. I suggested we bring him into the village to see Doctor O'Shea, but Jim wouldn't hear of it. Typical of your brother. More trust in the old ways.

How is life across the Atlantic? The children must be growing handsomely now. I would have liked to have seen them. I swear there'll only be me and Jim left in the county soon. Everyone seems to be packing up and heading off now, not so much to America but across to Liverpool, Manchester, Bolton and the likes. It's a funny world. But that's the state of the country. Worse it's getting. And I can't even joke about it with Jim, either, with the business and all. You and Donal were right to leave when you did.

I got the clipping you sent me – but honestly, Maud, it just wouldn't be possible to leave everything behind, not at our age. Jim is so wedded to the inn. Sometimes I think he loves it more than his family. I know it's a shocking thing to say, and I don't exactly have anyone else to say it to. It's not good to keep thoughts like that to oneself for too long. Perhaps you understand him better. Though it is nice to see jobs going over there. Maybe we can send some of the children over when they've grown a bit. There's not much for all six of them here.

I almost forgot to tell you – the priest called by this morning, just checking in and asking if we'd be all attending the Easter service. Yes – Father Maloney, God bless him. Must be seventy now. Of course, I invited him in for a cup of tea and... well, maybe it was because of that that he started asking about the children and what I was going to do, now that they're all at school. I said I was finally enjoying some peace and that I might do some cleaning up at the inn, just to help out, and he said, "a fine young woman such as yourself shouldn't be cleaning dusty old bedsheets."

"Young?" I laughed. I don't think you can call us young anymore! Bless him, I think he was trying to lift my spirits. And when he was leaving, he said the house was awfully quiet, and he asked if I was planning on having a few more. It was clear what he meant. I told him no, we were past that now. It's not me; I just don't think Jim's a bit interested, he's so preoccupied with the business.

I've got to run into the village now, before the children get home. Father Maloney's visit has me all flustered. At least it looks like the spring is here. The daffodils are up and there's a good long stretch in the evening. There's a bit of warmth in the air, too. It can only help Brendan – he doesn't do too well in the cold. He's not eating right after his last spell. No appetite at all. He's like a little fairy child. You wouldn't know of anything that would help? Not one of these 'old' cures, though. I should take him to the doctor if he gets poorly again, on my own accord. There are some things you can't burden a hardworking husband with. If you think of anything, let me know. I'll be on the lookout for your next letter – it can get awful lonely in these parts.

God bless!

Love,

Anne

IV

Rick, 2019

Castlestrange

I woke to the sun shining through the front window. My head was throbbing. *Brandy*, I remembered, as I sat up and rubbed my temples. But I hadn't drunk much. Perhaps I'd hit my head out on the roadside.

I could still see the hand in my mind. Long, white fingers stretching out. Brown, pointed nails. And the damaged, scarred skin, like it'd been burnt badly.

I reached for my phone on the coffee table. The screen looked even worse in daylight. I could barely see an app. I swiped the screen, but nothing happened. All I could see was the time: half-past ten. I could always get it fixed back in London, as I was trying not to use it here. Maybe this was a sign to focus on my detox. Focus on writing again.

After making a strong tea, I took a hot shower and changed into fresh clothes: a plaid shirt, which had a couple of buttons missing, but was cosy nonetheless, and a jacket. I felt slightly perkier, so I decided to pop into the village to pick up some groceries. I could also pick up a new cap as well.

The nearest village, Castlestrange, was barely a five-minute drive, not far from Castlestrange Lodge. However, I took a different, longer route, not wanting to pass the pub and possibly see Bertha. Twenty minutes later, I parked the car outside Castlestrange Stores on the bank of the River Suck.

I retrieved a small basket and spotted a few tweed caps hanging above raincoats and wellington boots in the corner. I dropped one in the basket.

The shop was quiet, luckily, giving me time to browse aimlessly after filling my basket, though I felt the shopkeeper's eyes on me. The place had a musty smell, and was probably several decades old. An abundance of fishing rods leant against the walls; not surprising, since the village was surrounded by rivers and lakes. I'd never been fishing on Black Lake before; in fact, I hadn't been fishing since moving to London. Should I spend the rest of the day fishing? I was on holiday, after all, and had the whole week to kill. There wasn't much else to do around here. I picked out the smallest and simplest-looking rod as well as some 'power lure' hooks, small toy fish that claimed to lure and catch live ones.

"Can I help you there?" the elderly shopkeeper asked from behind the counter.

"All good," I replied, then decided to pick up some wellington boots as well. I might as well go all out.

"Goin' fishin'?" he asked.

"Yes," I said. I kept my head down as I approached the till. I felt bare without my cap on. "Seems like the perfect day."

"We get a lot of tourists coming here to fish," he remarked as he rang up the old-fashioned cash register. He smelt of cigarettes.

"Bag?"

I nodded.

"There's some lovely rivers and lakes around," he said.

"I'm sure."

"That's 68.50." He pushed the bag towards me. "Where are

you staying?"

"Next to a lake, actually," I said, handing him my credit card. "Do you take card?"

He snatched the card from me, though he didn't seem pleased.

"Which lake is it?" he asked.

"Black Lake," I replied, my voice rising, making it sound more like a question than a statement.

"Oh yes," he murmured, handing back my card. "I know that one."

"Great. Well, thanks," I said, taking the fishing rod and wellington boots in hand and turning to leave.

"Wait!" he called.

I turned around to find him staring at me with piercing blue eyes, biting down on his lip.

"Yes?" I asked, hoping he hadn't realised who I was, like Mick and Bertha had.

"There are far better lakes for fishin'," he said. "Stoneham's Lake or Hollygrove Lake, or even the River Suck itself."

"Thanks." I smiled. "I'll have a look."

I left the shop wondering if there was some other reason behind his suggestion. I wasn't too fussed about actually catching fish, more wanting to enjoy the experience. But I couldn't help wondering if the shopkeeper also knew about Jim Harrow and where he'd thrown his burning body. Jim probably did set his house on fire, kill his family and throw himself in a lake due to extreme financial stress, but that didn't make the lake a place to avoid. People drowned in lakes all the time, surely.

I placed the new cap on my head, chucked the rod and groceries into the back seat and hopped into the car. There, sitting in the car in broad daylight, with the sound of children playing by the riverbank, it seemed ridiculous to have been scared by footsteps. My own footsteps, no doubt. Then there was the alcohol, of course, fuelling my imagination. It was the perfect mix to make me think I'd heard or seen something.

And the hand, Rick?

That was something I couldn't explain.

A buzz came from the passenger seat, rousing me from my thoughts. I glanced down and could just about see *Rach* below the cracked phone screen. I pressed the green icon, wondering if it would work.

"Yes?" I answered.

"Hi," she said in a quiet voice. "Am I interrupting you?"

"I told you I wouldn't be answering calls," I reminded her, perhaps too curtly. I'd told her not to disturb me this week. "In fact, my editor recommends it." That was a lie; I hadn't even listened to his voice messages yet. It was Bob Newport who'd advised against it.

"I know. I'm sorry. I just wanted to check if you'd made it okay."

"Almost." I tried to slow my breathing. I knew I shouldn't be so angry. She was only checking up.

"And have you been to the graveyard yet?"

"Later."

"Okay, I won't keep you, then."

"It'll just be one week," I reassured her. "I need to do this, for me. And to keep Pierce quiet."

"Of course. Goodbye, then."

"Goodbye."

"I love you, Rick."

I rarely became affectionate, but if this was the last phone call with her for the next several days, I might as well tell her.

"I love you too, Rachel."

I slipped the phone into my back pocket. Maybe I'd needed to hear that. One last phone call before I went full hermit. Could I go a week without hearing her voice? A week without a single message?

I turned the phone off. I had to commit to this digital detox. I hadn't handed in anything new to my editor for almost two years, and he desperately wanted a follow-up. Everyone at Caxton wanted a follow-up. But no one would allow me a break. I felt I just needed a break. A break from the expectation. A break from the pressure.

I backed out of the car park, trying to focus on the day ahead. This was my day, and I was going to make sure I enjoyed it.

Down by the Lake

It was only when I arrived at the cottage I realised I'd forgotten to pick up a new flowerpot for Brian. Soil had spread across the stones around the front door. I'd have to head to the shops again, but I was far too excited at the prospect of spending the afternoon angling on the lake to go back now.

I threw on Brian's raincoat and fetched the rod before heading down to the pier, having decided I'd put the groceries away later. There were a couple of boats sitting on either side of the pier. I hoped I could borrow one, despite having not seen anyone around the lake that day or the day before. Perhaps it was well known that the lake was haunted, or cursed, or maybe November was the wrong time to go fishing. Whatever the case, there was no one around to see me take a boat.

I hopped inside and untied the rope. I picked up the wooden paddle and, thrusting it against the pier, pushed the boat out into the lake. Though the water was still, the boat rocked, doubtless due to my inefficient paddling. The lake wasn't vast, but still substantial, maybe fifteen or twenty acres. It was enough to keep me close to the shore – it wasn't that I couldn't swim, but in case it suddenly got dark; the sun was already descending. I'd forgotten how early it became dark in the countryside, with no artificial lights.

The lake was eerily quiet. I shivered and pulled down my cap. The air had turned chilly. I swung the fishing rod in the air and the toy bait landed in the water with a plop, causing a ripple in the otherwise still water. Despite the clear sky and golden rays of the setting sun, the surface was as black as ever. I began to wonder if there were any fish in the lake at all – if the shopkeeper was right and I was wasting my time. But I wasn't out here to actually catch fish, I reminded myself – there was plenty of food in the cottage for dinner. I was here to relax, unwind, take in the serene surroundings, and forget all about London, my editor, and my readers. Leave all their needs behind. Have some 'me time', at last.

Was that selfish of me? To leave them all behind, even Rachel, for a holiday? What did they think? Hadn't my editor targets to hit? A job to keep? And now it was November, and I was sitting in a boat in the centre of a lake in the middle of nowhere with a rod in my hands, pretending to fish.

What the hell am I doing?

Furious with myself, I yanked the rod, only to find the hook stuck. I pulled again, but it wouldn't budge. I clamped the rod between my legs and paddled closer, wondering if I should just abandon it. But I wasn't a litterbug, and leaving a big plastic rod at the bottom of a lake would be the ultimate twenty-first century transgression. So, I paddled towards the stuck hook, desperate to yank it free. But as I leaned over the edge of the boat, I saw something black ahead of me: a shape standing on the shore amongst the trees, facing me. The figure appeared to be wearing a long dark-coloured coat and a brown hat. Their head was bowed, as if they were looking at their shoes, making it impossible to see their face. Had they too come to fish?

The string lurched. I pulled, but the hook seemed to be still caught. When I pulled harder, it suddenly came free, making me lose my balance. I fell backwards, landing on the small of my back, and causing the boat to rock. I kept a firm grip on the rod but found myself propelled to my feet. Something heavy was pulling it away. I yanked the rod, lifting a giant, silver fish from the water. The fish, presumably a pike, was two or three feet long and incredibly heavy, bending the rod to such an angle I thought it might snap. I hoped to manoeuvre it into the boat, where I could then untangle the string and unleash the fish, but it was flopping so much it somehow released itself, falling into the water with a massive splash. I was relieved to see it go, but I was still fired up with adrenaline.

I was astonished; I hadn't expected to catch a fish, let alone a huge one. Maybe I wasn't so useless after all.

I glanced in the direction of the figure to see if they'd seen my catch, only to find nobody there.

I collapsed back into the boat, panting heavily. My heart was racing, my hands trembling. I'd actually caught a fish, and I had no way of texting Rachel. But perhaps a broken phone was the best for this detox.

I couldn't help my gaze returning to the spot where the person had stood. What had they been looking at?

Me?

Then I remembered Brian's story, and heard his voice in my head: *He emerged from the front door in flames ... before running down the field and throwing himself in the lake.*

Was Jim's body still floating below me, his ghost walking above?

I shook my head and picked up the paddle, wanting to return to the shore, before I got carried away by my overactive imagination.

The sun had almost set, the sky turning an inky blue. I wanted to dock the boat as quickly as possible, especially if there were people around. As I paddled back to the pier, I discerned a light beaming from the dark. I squinted my eyes. It was coming in the direction of the cottage.

It must be a car, I thought. Maybe the person I'd seen standing by the trees was leaving.

As I neared the pier, I realised it wasn't a car light: it was the motion-sensor light from the cottage. But it wasn't the light that made me freeze.

Somebody was standing outside the cottage, looking in my direction.

Like Old Times

After tying up the boat, I hurried up to the cottage, my hand held above my eyes. The bright outdoor light was blinding. *Someone must want to talk to me,* I thought. *Maybe they wanted their boat back.*

"Hello?" I called, unable to see properly. I continued in the direction of the cottage nonetheless, hoping not to bump into them. When I made it to the door eventually, I looked around, but couldn't see anyone. I glanced around the corner of the cottage, but there were only trees. Still, I went around to the other side, just in case. There was no one there either. Whoever had been standing outside the cottage, watching me, had already left.

Had it been the same figure? I turned the key and headed inside, thinking. Maybe someone had been trying to confront me for taking their boat, but then had decided it wasn't worth it. Or it was just a nosy neighbour, checking who was staying at the cottage. But then they would have stuck around. Besides, there weren't too many neighbours out here, if any. This was the only cottage I'd seen around the lake.

I kicked off my boots and flicked on the lights.

Something shimmered on the floor. I peered down to see patches of water, all the way to the bathroom. It took me a few moments to register that they looked like the outlines of shoes, as if someone had worn their wet shoes inside.

"Hello?" I called. There was no answer. I headed down the hall to the bathroom, manoeuvring around the wet shoe tracks to check if I'd opened the window after my shower earlier. "Hello?" I asked again, tapping gently on the door.

There was no answer. I pushed down on the handle and opened the door slowly. Through the narrow chink I saw a pair of bright, blue eyes looking out behind a mass of messy, brown hair.

My hair.

I gazed into my own eyes. When my awareness returned, I threw my hands over my eyes and pushed myself back into the hall, collapsing into the wall. Getting to my feet, I dashed to the bedroom for a towel.

I ran back to the bathroom, towel in hand, and threw it over the mirror. Then I hurried into the hall and peered into the living room. The mirror was still facing the wall. I breathed a sigh of relief.

Relax, Rick.

I stepped back and took a deep breath, focusing my thoughts. Someone had taken the towel from the bathroom mirror. But why? And how had they got in?

I returned to the bathroom to check the window, now that the mirror was safely covered. It was closed, as I had expected. I looked around for the missing towel but couldn't find it anywhere. Somebody must have taken it down. Someone had somehow broken into the cottage and removed the towel from the mirror.

Why would anyone want to do that?

After locking the front door and door to the back kitchen, I headed to the living room and fell onto the couch.

Should I phone the Guards? Over the towel?

Now, I really wished I'd bought a new bottle of brandy from the shop. Though that would probably have made me even more confused.

I'm sober. I can figure this out.

No one breaks into a house to steal a towel. Brian had obviously used it last night.

He'd pulled me out of a ditch. Of course I must have been covered in dirt.

I sat up, racking my brain. It had been taken innocently. But where had he put it? He hadn't mentioned taking a towel away to be washed. Had he put it in the washing machine?

I made for the kitchen and opened the washing machine door. It was empty. Had he taken it with him? That would be an odd thing to do. Or was something else going on? Was someone really trying to mess with me?

Mick and his nephews?

It must be, I thought as I gazed through the blackened kitchen window. It had to be them. They'd scared me last night. And now that they knew where I was, they were continuing their fun. I suppose there wasn't much excitement for them around here. A writer arrives from London, staying on his own in the middle of nowhere, practically begging to be pranked. This was their final trick.

But how had they got in?

I found myself staring into the murky darkness. The outdoor light had turned off. The lake was nowhere in sight. Just an empty, black void. It was rare to find yourself in such darkness, especially in London. There was always a streetlight beaming outside the window. Wasn't this what I wanted? Complete, utter darkness? Complete silence? Away from Pierce's calls and emails? ~~Even away from Rachel?~~

[Note to editor: delete last thought]

The outside light activated. I peered out of the window, but couldn't see anyone. The only movement was the gentle sway of branches closest to me. Even the water was still.

A knock sounded. I jumped, startled. The cottage was a state: dirty boots, groceries waiting to be put away, and the floor now wet. I headed to the door.

A man stood on the porch, his back to me.

"Brian?" I asked.

"Yes," he answered, turning around. "I thought you might be out – I was just about to leave." As he took a step towards me, I stepped back. He was wearing a long dark-brown coat over his tweed jacket and a matching, slightly battered hat.

The same as the figure by the trees?

"I see you've found your cap," he commented, a smile creasing his smooth skin.

"No." I shook my head. "It's a new one. Bought it from the shop. Is there something you need?" I asked, holding the door firmly.

Why is he here?

"Oh, no." He reached inside his coat. "Just thought I'd grab another bottle, after I drank most of it last night."

He produced a tall bottle of brandy and handed it to me.

"Thank you," I said, taking it, relieved to know why he'd come. I'd been only seconds away from asking if he'd been watching me by the lake. "You didn't have to."

"I thought you might need something after the shock of last night. I can't say I helped, filling your head with nonsense stories."

His eyes drifted to the soil and shards covering the ground.

"Oh, I'll buy a new one," I said quickly. "A new pot, I mean. Sorry about that."

"That's alright. I've got plenty at the house. You might just want to give it a sweep."

"Of course."

"Lovely, well, if there's anything you need, do give me a shout. I'm only up the road."

"I will," I said. Then I asked, "You haven't seen a towel, actually?"

"A towel?"

"It's just that a towel disappeared from my bathroom." I realised how stupid I sounded. It was just a towel, after all. "Never mind. I'm sure it will turn up."

"If there aren't enough towels, I can always bring some over in the morning."

"No, no, it's alright." I didn't want to make this more than it was. "There's plenty. Thank you again."

"Right." He nodded. "I'll leave you to enjoy your evening then. Good night, Mister Mulrooney."

"Good night."

I closed the door. I'd really wanted to ask if he'd been down by the lake earlier, but I'd sounded silly enough asking about a missing towel. He was probably just out walking. Or he had come to give me the brandy earlier, when I wasn't here. There was nothing else to it.

But what about the footprints?

I placed the bottle on the table and hung up my raincoat – Brian's raincoat, I realised. I'd completely forgotten to give it back, being so preoccupied with a stupid towel. I'd have to return it later.

I retrieved a mop from the back kitchen. To my surprise, when I emerged from the kitchen, the floor was completely dry. Leaning the mop against the wall, I got to my knees, running my fingers over the wood. Bone dry.

Not a drop.

Not even a mark.

How had it dried that fast?

I returned the unused mop and once again ensured the door was locked.

What was going on? Had someone come inside, wet the floor, then mopped it up while I wasn't looking? That was absurd. Or had it just dried naturally?

After finally putting the shopping away and popping a ready-made meal in the microwave, I retrieved a glass from the cupboard and took it to the worktop. I thought I deserved a drink after all the strange happenings, maybe even a large one.

In the living room I sank into the couch. Taking a sip of the brandy, I began to think.

The man on the lake edge was Brian, out for a walk. Possibly coming to see me. Realising I wasn't home, he'd left. He then saw the lights turning on, and returned to check. But the footprints? That had to have been me. I'd put the groceries down inside, after all. I then went down the hall after coming home, to use the bathroom, even if I couldn't remember it. I supposed it was such a mundane thing, using the bathroom – our brains decide not to store that information. We don't normally remember each and every time we've gone to the bathroom. And the floor had dried naturally, like all floors do.

There was still the towel, though. I'd probably knocked it off the mirror after using the bathroom, on my way out. But where had it gone? Had I dragged it somewhere with my feet, without knowing? Possibly – but then it should be somewhere in the cottage.

Placing my glass on the coffee table, I got up to check on my dinner. I should be enjoying myself, not worrying excessively about a missing towel. This was my holiday. My 'me time'.

So that's what I did, at least for that evening. With a book and bottle in hand, I headed to bed.

Like old times.

△

I distinctly remember sensing someone in my room. I opened my eyes, glancing at the time on my phone through the cracked screen: 02:20.

I peered over the bedsheets, hoping to see Rachel. But in her place was a long, black silhouette standing at the foot of my bed and wearing a hat. Their head was slightly bowed.

Cold sweat formed on my forehead. My hands and feet felt like they were turning to ice. I wanted to pull my knees to my chest, but I couldn't move a single limb.

They didn't move, continuing to stare at their feet, or the floor. What were they doing? What did they want? I wanted to ask, but I failed to make a sound. My mouth was dry, my tongue stuck to its roof. I tried to move it, but it wouldn't budge. It was completely stuck. It was like being frozen in a dream, unable to move, unable to speak.

I watched the figure, though I wanted to look away. Waves of fear radiated through my body, and with each intense wave I could hear a ringing in my ears. It felt like it was coming from the figure. And somehow, I knew they wanted to harm me.

The figure raised his right arm. They were holding something. Some kind of container. Gloved hands were clenched around a handle. A canister, I realised. They turned the vessel upwards, tilting it, and I heard liquid spilling on the carpeted floor.

Then his name came to me.

Jim Harrow.

No! I screamed in my head as he dropped the empty canister onto the floor. Next, he reached into his coat. I heard the quick scratch of a match and for a moment the room was bathed in a red-orange glow.

No!

He raised his arm again, his head still bowed. The flame flickered, casting his long shadow against the door behind him. The fear swelled in my body, the cold, clammy sweat wetting the sheets.

This is it, I realised. *I'm going to die.*

The match dropped from his fingers.

The room was nothing but light.

V

Anne, 1939

Letters from Anne Harrow to Maud Kavanagh

Fairy Hill
12th April 1939

Dear Maud,

I received your letter with your warnings. I have to say I was a little surprised, although Jim is also of a similar mind.

On Holy Thursday we all trekked into the village, even Jim. I was so pleased the inn was closed for a few days, and it was nice to be out as a whole family for once. At least, that's what I thought before we attended mass.

I took Brendan to the front of the church, to the front pew. I thought a wash of the feet would help strengthen him. I'd discussed it earlier in the week when Father Maloney called. It can't do any harm to be blessed. Well, I never heard a child of four scream so loud! The moment the water wet his feet, he kicked and wailed, as if it was boiling water pouring on his skin. Father Maloney had an awful fright, which isn't good for someone his age. Jim looked furious in the front pew, his face glowing red. I tried to ease Brendan but he just would not stop. Screaming and screaming. Jim wasn't taking any of it. He stood up and yanked the poor child from my arms, then marched him down the church and out the door, barefoot and all. Oh Maud, I was so embarrassed. I didn't know what to do. The whole church was looking at me. I couldn't help but think – what have I done to deserve this?

You can see I am trembling as I recount this. It was awful. Mortified, I gathered Brendan's socks and shoes and hurried after them, the children following. Jim was dragging poor Brendan down the road, the child balling. I couldn't stop him. I begged and begged but Jim was in one of his moods. His eyes wouldn't budge from Brendan, as if he was determined to make this child suffer. When I tried to put Brendan's socks on, he pulled the child away. Surely it wasn't the child's fault? The water must have been freezing cold and he probably had a shock. But I don't know how to reason with your brother when he's in one of those dark moods.

Brendan's feet were all red and sore by the time we got home, and I had to run a lukewarm bath to ease them. Jim headed straight to the inn, to whatever it was he needed there. I was glad to be rid of him, to be honest. Now you tell me what could be wrong with him, and don't mention any of this fairy magic. You know what Jim said when he came home hours later, the smell of whiskey on his breath? You won't believe it. He said it wasn't Doctor O'Shea Brendan needed, but a fairy doctor. A fairy doctor! Whatever in God's name that is, I don't know, but what I do know is I'll make sure no fairy doctor comes into this house. That's what I said to Jim. He thinks Brendan is under some sort of spell, that he must have been out one night on the hill and visited by fairies. I didn't even know there was a fairy rath on our own land, but I do now. Jim won't stop going on about it. I suppose that's where the place gets its name.

And I suppose you agree with your brother. I don't know why you both do, but I don't believe in any of this fairy nonsense. I'm sorry, but it's true. I'll go back to the church to see what Father Maloney has to say. I'm sure he'll advise to see the doctor – a proper doctor. Fairy doctors and fairy raths – I can't understand it, not in this day and age. It's like something our grandparents would say.

And I don't fully understand your warnings about the month of May, and I don't want to ask Jim. I won't be letting Brendan anywhere near the fairy rath or the water on the first Monday of May, although I'm not sure what there is to be afraid of. It's not the hill or the water to be concerned about, but Brendan's worsening health. And how are primroses plucked before sunrise supposed to help? I suppose the girls will enjoy gathering them and scattering them about the place, and it will be a nice gesture to welcome the spring. If it helps ease your nerves, we won't be letting Brendan out much at all, never mind near the water!

I wonder if something happened when Jim was young – you'd tell me, Maud, wouldn't you? I don't like not knowing what could be bothering Jim. He's awful sullen, especially now after Thursday's episode. We decided to leave Brendan at home for the rest of the week. I don't know if that's right, but I'll see what Father Maloney has to say.

Send my love to Donal and all. God bless!

Love,

Anne

△

Fairy Hill
22nd June 1939

Dear Maud,

Sorry I didn't write to you all of May. It's been a strange few weeks. There's no improvement in Brendan. Jim's fully convinced it's due to the fairy folk – he never leaves the bedroom window at night, looking out at the fairy rath, afraid they'll come and take his son.

There were bonfires lit all around the countryside last night, glowing from every field and hill for the Summer Solstice. We could hear music and singing all night, and Jim swears he saw fairy folk dancing on the rath. But there's always been music and dancing on Bonfire Night – that's what I tell him, but he won't listen to me. I don't know what goes on inside his head, but he seems very absent, like his mind is somewhere else. Almost as if he himself is away with the fairies!

The girls and I scattered the primroses around the threshold, and hung garlands on the front and back doors. I don't know what good it will do, but at least the girls seemed to enjoy it. I'm more inclined to give in to Jim's notions and seek this fairy doctor now, prove to you and your brother it's nonsense, then get on with taking Brendan to a real doctor.

So you see, Maud, I am taking your advice, even if I don't agree with it. If I knew the truth, perhaps I might be more open-minded. Are these fairy beings you and your brother talk so much about honestly a danger to Brendan? Or is it something else? Is there something else far more sinister in these parts other than fairies that could harm Brendan? I must assume you'd tell me, as your sister-in-law and mother to your brother's children. You will tell me, won't you? Did something happen to you and Jim here?

If you don't tell me, Maud, I may not be able to fully protect our son from harm. I can't trust Jim, and to be honest, I don't think the drinking helps. But you've always been sensible, like the older sister I never had, and I have followed all your advice. So I beg you once again Maud, please tell me. For Brendan's sake.

God bless!

Love,
Anne

VI

Rick, 2019

All Souls' Day

I sprang upright, gasping for air. I was soaked in sweat and the bedsheets clung to my skin. It was still dark. I couldn't detect any smoke. I turned on the bedside lamp and peered over the bottom of the bed. The carpet was completely unblemished. There were no markings on a wall. No sign a fire had been lit.

It must have been a dream, I thought.

I picked up my phone. It had just gone six am. I hadn't slept much, then, staying up much later than I'd intended, reading my book and, judging by the half-empty bottle on the bedside table, enjoying Brian's brandy.

The dream had seemed so real. So vivid. And I still sensed the presence. I don't how to explain it rationally, but I didn't feel safe in the room that morning.

I sat back against the headboard, running a hand through my damp, messy hair. I'd never get back to sleep, not after being so frightened. I grabbed the bottle and got up, my head whirling slightly, making my stomach dizzy. *It must have been the brandy,* I thought. I never had restful sleep after drinking, even if it did knock me out for a couple of hours at first. And Rach said I shouldn't drink. I stumbled out of the bedroom and down the hall. It would be the last time I'd drink again, I decided, as I hid the bottle in the cupboard.

I made a coffee in the largest mug I could find, adding an extra spoonful for a much-needed kick. I tugged the mug close to me, as if it was a comforting toy, then peered through the window. It was still dark outside, the blackness thick.

After a long shower switching between hot and cold water – I was in much need of stimulation that morning – I dressed and took the car into the village. It was 2nd November, and I thought it best to pay my parents a visit for All Souls' Day. I wasn't going to visit the graveyard empty-handed again, so I thought I'd pick up a nice bunch of flowers.

Everything appeared normal – it was another crisp and sunny morning, cold but not bitter. I had an urge to phone Rachel, to check she was okay; the dream had felt like a threat, or warning, and made me think about her. I shook my head, deciding it'd be best not to disturb her; she'd only be alarmed, thinking her horror-writer husband was now suffering from harrowing premonitions. Besides, I wasn't sure if my banjaxed phone could even make calls.

The riverbank was busier than the day before: there were a couple of families sitting at the picnic tables, and children dunking fishing nets into the water. Two boys bounced up and down on a seesaw and a couple of girls were gently swaying on the swing beside it, singing to themselves.

I put on my gloves and got out of the car. As I made my way to the shop door, the children's singing grew louder, carried on the breeze. I could hear their words clearly, and listened, as I thought the words sounded strange:

Over the hill, down by the lake,
The water's dark and murky
And if you look just past the reeds

You'll find the fairies lurkin'.

They sing and dance with wild romance
All through the night and morning,
Be careful not to wander near
They'll take you with no warning.

With wicked grins and eyes so white
they travel through their portal
To be amongst their kings and queens
and gift their new immortal.

So tread with caution, little one,
And beware the mystic call
For over the hill, down by the lake,
The fairies charm us all.

As I opened the door, the singing faded. I peered over my shoulder: a young boy and girl were sitting on the seesaw, and the girls on the swings had their backs turned to me.

Down by the lake? I thought. *Did I hear them correctly?*

"Are ya comin' in?" a voice boomed, waking me from my thoughts. It was the shopkeeper, watching me from behind the counter. "You'll have us all catch our death," he warned. It was only then I realised I was still holding the door open.

"You don't have any flowers, do you?" I asked.

"Wrong shop," the shopkeeper growled, as if I'd insulted him. "You'll have to head into town for the likes of that."

His jaw clenched and his two big hands made into fists on his hips.

I noticed all the bottles gleaming on the shelves behind him.

Perhaps I should pick up a bottle for Brian, in case he calls again...

"Just a bottle of brandy, then," I said, closing the door behind me.

△

Exiting the shop, and with 40 euros less in my wallet, I listened for singing but could only hear the rushing of the river. When I looked up, I realised there were no children there at all. The swings were completely still. The seesaw was abandoned. I scanned up and down the riverbank, but there was no child to be seen. Had I imagined them, as well as the singing?

Only the parents remained, sitting around the picnic tables, sipping their drinks. Then I realised they didn't look like parents exactly, more like teenagers, drinking from green- and red-coloured cans, possibly cider. They couldn't be parents, surely? I watched as one guzzled theirs before tossing the empty can on the grass. I was surprised I hadn't noticed their ripped jeans and hoodies masking their eyes. I suppose I hadn't really been paying attention, distracted by the song. Or perhaps the parents had fled when the binge-drinking teens descended, thinking it was no longer safe? Whatever the case, these cheap cider-guzzling teens definitely weren't parents.

"Rick?" a faint voice said.

I turned to see a grey-haired woman huddled in a large red coat, standing by a car. It was open, her gloved hand clenched around the edge. It took me a good few seconds to realise who it was. Her hair had greyed considerably and the sunlight caught some streaks of white. She seemed thinner too, despite the large coat. It was so large, in fact, and heavy-looking, that it seemed to be forcing her to stoop. Her face was long and gaunt, the sharp cheekbones creating dark hollows where plump, rosy cheeks had been.

"Carol?" I moved closer. She stood firmly behind the car door, eyeing me. "Oh, wow – how have you been?" I asked, wondering if that was the right thing to say or if it only underscored my shock at her appearance.

"Surviving," she replied matter-of-factly. She barely moved, except for her hand tightening around the car door.

"Sure." I wondered what to say next. I had rarely been alone with Rachel's mother, and when I had, she would do all the talking. It wasn't a secret she was far from in awe at my career. "How's Peter?" I asked.

"The same," she said, her eyes narrowing.

I wasn't sure if she meant *the same as me* or *the same as ever*, so I just nodded and smiled. "Good," I said finally, wondering if she'd always been this distant. "It's not a bad day."

"What are you doing here, Rick?" she asked. Her gaze dropped to the bottle in my hand. *Shit! Why did she have to see me now?* Her eyes moved up and down, inspecting me. This was the worst possible time she could see me: tired, alone, a big bottle of brandy in my hand. I hadn't even put it in a bag.

"I'm just visiting," I replied finally, attempting to stuff the bottle into my back pocket but failing miserably. "Stop off at the graveyard. Clear my mind, you know?"

She didn't respond. Didn't even nod. She just continued to stare at me. I must have looked an absolute wreck. Should I add that I needed to write a new book by January? That I was having writer's block and needed inspiration?

I noticed the rims of her eyes were red. I caught a whiff of flowery perfume, reminding me of Rachel's house. The Kelly house always smelt floral. I had sometimes wondered if Carol went about the house spraying it with perfume.

"Will you be going back?" she asked, breaking the silence.

"Yes, next week," I replied, even though I hadn't actually booked a return flight. I hadn't been sure if one week would be enough.

She looked at the shop door uneasily.

"The shopkeeper is friendly," I joked, but her expression didn't change. Her thin lips were as hard as stone. "I'd better head to the graveyard," I added.

She nodded, and her gaze dropped again. Now she seemed to be studying my knitted, fingerless gloves. She must have thought I was on the streets, or a hipster.

"It's chilly," I gasped, tugging my free hand under my arm.

I thought she was about to say something, but she only closed the car door, then clicked the key fob. The car beeped. Donning her sunglasses, she headed towards the shop.

"Take care of yourself, Rick."

Distractions

I reversed the car, not wanting to linger. Carol had clearly been surprised to see me. Unnerved, even. Had I scared her? Did she think I was drunk? Perhaps there was something Rachel wasn't telling me.

With Carol's sudden appearance, I'd almost forgotten about the song. It drifted into my head once I was out on the main road. The words had referred to a lake, and dark water. Could that be Black Lake? It was probably just a song to keep children away from water, and I just happened to be staying next to a lake called Black Lake. Still, I thought it was an odd song for children to sing, and had a strange effect on me. The skin on my arms crawled just thinking about it. It must be a playground chant or folk-song. Is that normal of today's children, to sing these archaic-sounding songs? Rachel and I have been discussing having a child for years. A child is something we both want, but we're waiting for the right time. Or, more precisely, I'm waiting for the right time. Maybe that's why Carol doesn't like me.

I wasn't paying attention when a car suddenly swerved out in front of me. I hit the brake. A horn sounded. The car continued driving, gathering speed before vanishing around a hill.

My heart hammered in my chest. I looked around to see where I was: outside a pub next to the graveyard. The car had been coming from the graveyard and the driver hadn't seen me around the sharp bend.

I let the car crawl slowly towards the pub and came to a stop outside, then rolled down the window for some air; I was still panting after the speeding car and I was feeling lightheaded.

I'd told Rachel we were in no state to start a family – not yet, anyway. I don't exactly have a bestseller under my belt, but I'd once had a steady income, publishing one, even two books a year. I'd tried to explain we should be more financially stable before having kids, even buy a house with a mortgage beside a good school. But a mortgage would require having a salaried job, and potentially quitting writing altogether. Despite having submitted dozens of applications, I'd never even had the chance to speak to a mortgage advisor, even after I'd received a substantial advance that would make up a large portion of the deposit. They didn't seem to consider writing as a real profession, and no amount of freelancing would ever persuade them. Even Rachel's permanent job in marketing wouldn't cut it. I'd promised her I'd start looking for a salaried job, write my novels part-time – I'm not sure how I'd tell Pierce that! I know Rachel's not happy about it. "Someday," I'd told her. That was almost two years ago.

I rolled up the window, thinking about Rachel's mother, and the strange song. And now, almost being hit by a car, all in the same morning. And then there was the figure standing by the lake, watching. Down by a lake, where the water is dark, and fairies can be seen and heard. Was that not Black Lake? Why couldn't it be? But it wasn't a fairy I'd seen; it was a tall man in a coat and hat.

As I turned the key in the ignition, my phone rang. I glanced down at the cracked screen: *Rach.*

Shit!

Had Carol phoned her already? Told her how awful I looked? That I was drinking again?

"Yes?" I said into the phone.

There was a muffled sound on the end of the line. Then she said in a soft voice, "Hello."

"Did Carol call?"

"Mammy?" she asked, surprised. "Oh, no, she hasn't. I haven't heard from her, no. Why?"

"I just bumped into her," I explained. "In Castlestrange. She seemed, I don't know, a bit off. Distant. Like she wasn't fully there. Is she alright, do you know?"

"I think so. I mean, I haven't heard from her in a while, but I'm sure I'd know if there was a problem. Joan keeps a close eye on them."

"Anyway, you've caught me at a bad time, Rachel," I told her.

She inhaled. "Oh, I'm sorry."

"You know I'm still doing this detox."

"I know, sorry," she murmured. "I just wanted to check up. I'll try and get through to Mam, see if anything's going on." She paused. "Have you been to the graveyard yet?"

"No. In fact, I was just about to go there now. Thought I'd pick up some flowers first."

"Of course. That's nice of you. When can I call again?"

"I don't know," I replied. *Maybe I shouldn't go to the graveyard,* I thought. *The flowers can wait.*

"Rick, are you still there?" Rachel asked.

"Yes, but I have to go."

"Is something wrong?"

"No, nothing's wrong."

"Okay. I'll call at a better time, then."

"No!"

In the silence that followed, I tried to regain my composure. "Look, just give it a few days. Or a week."

"Rick…" she began.

"I've got to go."

"Rick—"

"Goodbye, Rachel."

"Rick!"

"Goodbye!"

~~I slammed the phone on the passenger seat. Why did she always call at the worst moments? Always distracting me. This was why I hadn't done any writing in the past year. Maybe *she* was the distraction.~~

[Note to editor: please delete previous paragraph]

I sat back. Tried to calm down. There'd been too many distractions: the tall figure, Carol, and now this song, warning me to stay away from a lake. And didn't the shopkeeper warn against it too? Is there something about Black Lake that I don't know? Whatever the case, I'd never write anything here. I needed somewhere where I couldn't just bump into my girlfriend's parents whenever I popped into the village. Somewhere I wasn't being watched.

And had I even dreamt about a figure watching me from the foot of my bed? Who had that been? Who was trying to scare me?

Brian?

My foot pressed hard on the accelerator. I couldn't stop the thoughts coming. Why had he appeared just after I'd heard the footsteps on the road? Just after I spotted the figure by the lake? Just after I found the cottage broken into?

Brian had been acting strange, practically stalking me, checking up for no apparent reason. And then there were the shoe tracks on the cottage floor. Had that been him too? Couldn't he have let himself in, at any time? Watched me in my sleep?

My foot pressed hard on the accelerator. What was he up to? Was he trying to scare me? Why hadn't I questioned him before?

At last, I spotted the Guinness sign on Castlestrange Lodge through the trees and kept my foot firmly pressed on the accelerator. I should have left this place already.

It wasn't fairies haunting Black Lake: it was Brian.

VII

Pierce, 2020

Email from Pierce Rowlandson to Julia Crouch

From: pierce rowlandson <pierce.rowlandson@caxtonpublishing.com>
Sent: Wednesday, January 1, 2020 4:10 PM
To: julia.crouch@caxtonpublishing.com
Subject: Rick

Julia,

He's much worse than I thought. Completely unresponsive. He just gazed out the window the whole time I sat there, like he was looking for something, or could see something. And his eyes – eerily vacant. Even up close, he doesn't register me. There's just reflection. It's bad, Julia. Really bad.

I've read the manuscript. Well, most of it. Rick's handwriting is poor but I've had to read many handwritten manuscripts in my early commissioning days. Unfortunately, a stern nurse with a clipboard came around to announce the end of visiting hours and, though I tried to skim to the end, returned to usher me from the room. "We'll be giving Rick his dinner shortly," she told me as she led me from the ward. I wished her my luck.

I considered returning the journal and the stack of letters to Rick's satchel, but I didn't want to risk any other visitor walking in and taking them, so I've put them in my laptop bag for now.

I can't decide if Rick's manuscript is mostly fact or fiction, or if he's simply used his digital detox and the cottage as a base for this fantastical story. Did he *really* play with a spirit board in that pub? Did a bulb actually explode, a hand appear out of the fog? And who had entered the cottage? It must be fictionalised, surely. Or at least these elements are.

And does he truly think I'm such a nuisance? Has he ever complained about me, do you know? I basically launched his writing career. One of the first authors I signed up as part of my new imprint at Caxton & Co. And I email him at most once a week, just to check in. It's touching how he trusts me to delete his feelings about Rachel, though. I don't think I will. And to be honest, I don't think he'll ever know, not if he remains a vegetable forever. And bumping into Rachel's mother? That sat oddly with me. Why would Rick include that?

I'm back in the hospital café again, tinkering with this email. It's a little quieter now. I simply have to continue reading Rick's MS, so I'm keeping this email brief. Almost at the end!

I'll email you once I'm finished.

Kind regards,

Pierce

PS haven't found my cute nurse yet :'(

VIII

Rick, 2019

A Road Blocked

The moment I reached the cottage, I jumped out of the car and ran inside, ready to pack.

I flung the wardrobe doors open and threw clothes into my suitcase. I didn't bother clearing the bathroom as I was so desperate to leave: Brian could chuck my things, I didn't care. In the living room, I glanced out of the window. There was no sign of Brian, or anyone else. No one was visiting the lake today.

I locked the front door, unsure where to leave the keys: the pot was broken, and I realised I hadn't yet swept the porch. *Too late now,* I thought. I crouched to slip the key under a broken shard. Then I dragged the suitcase down the steps before tossing it into the back seat of the car.

The engine was still running as I got in. I'd have to find somewhere else to stay that night, I realised. It was still early morning, so I was in luck. I picked up my phone, forgetting it was damaged. *Useless,* I thought, flinging it on the passenger seat. I didn't even have my laptop. I'd have to drive into town, find a computer café – if they still existed – or use the library.

I hit the accelerator, watching the cottage disappear in the side-view mirror, hoping it was the last time I saw it. I drove over the bridge, hopefully for the last time too, and remembered the fog that had blinded me there. It was lucky I hadn't fallen from that height, into the river below.

Just as I was approaching Castlestrange Lodge, I saw two men in high-visibility vests standing on a junction, signalling me to stop. I couldn't understand why; there were no signs of an accident. I slowed the car, crawling towards the door of the pub, where several people were standing. They had their backs turned to me, watching the two men in the high-vis vests.

I pulled up the handbrake. What were they all looking at?

As I felt my anger bubbling, a long black hearse slowly emerged from the road to the left and turned in the direction of Castlestrange. Behind it was another black hearse, not quite so big, also driving in the same direction. Two hearses. Two deaths.

I continued watching, the engine running, when another black hearse appeared. Three deaths? A regular car followed, and then another, and another. A funeral procession.

I turned the engine off, my anger subsiding, and bowed my head. Whatever had happened must have been tragic. Three deaths, possibly from the same family. I kept my head bowed for a few minutes.

When I looked up, I spotted another figure, standing on the corner behind the procession. They wore the same brown hat and long, dark coat I'd seen the person wearing who stood on the lake shore. Possibly the same hat and coat I'd seen Brian wearing. I wasn't an expert on hats, but I think it was a trilby. I couldn't see their face properly from such a distance, and the passing cars obstructed my view.

Could that be Brian?

I turned the engine back on so I could park the car and hurry to catch up to him. As I edged closer to the pub, the figure turned and walked in the direction the cars were coming from. When I'd finally parked the car, the procession had ended, and the figure had disappeared.

The bystanders outside the pub turned around, some nodding towards me sombrely, before heading inside.

I grabbed my phone, locked the car and hurried towards the road, afraid I'd lose sight of Brian. I wanted to get some answers from him about his intrusions. Just as I passed the pub car park, I spotted Bertha getting out of a jeep. I averted my gaze towards the road, hoping she wouldn't see me. Her quick footsteps crunched on the gravel. But then the sound stopped.

"You have some nerve," I heard her say coolly. "Showing up here, and those three men dead."

I continued walking, attempting to ignore her.

"That's it, keep on walking. Wouldn't want you to kill any more of my customers."

I halted, turning to look at her. Her face and bulbous cheeks were glowing red. A bunch of keys dangled in her hand.

"What do you mean, kill?" I asked. "I haven't..."

Three hearses.

Three men.

"I didn't..."

Mick.

Tom.

Adam.

"Get out of my sight," she hissed. "I'll have to get this whole place exorcised because of you. And how is it that *you're* still alive? Why didn't he take you?"

"Okay," I said slowly, trying to keep my composure. It'd be best to get away from her quickly. But I couldn't help asking:

"What happened?"

"Tractor accident. On that very road," she stated, pointing a key in the direction of the road junction. "It's a bad road; always has been. But it wasn't the road that killed them. I've never seen the likes, and on All Saints as well. The whole tractor went up in flames. I'm surprised you didn't see the smoke." Her eyes narrowed, as she looked me up and down.

"No, I didn't," I said, stunned. Before turning, I asked, "Do you know any landlord named Brian around here? He owns the cottage I'm staying in, a cottage by Black Lake."

She rolled her eyes when I mentioned the lake, before murmuring "Brian," under her breath.

"Yes," I said. "Late fifties, or early sixties. Wears a hat."

"There are more than a few Brians around here," she said, turning the keys in her fingers. "But I don't know any landlords named Brian."

"He said he lives up the road from me," I explained. "I assume this way, as it's only forest on the other side."

"Look, I haven't a clue. Try some of the houses on that road there." She pointed to the road from where the procession emerged.

"Thanks," I said. "I'll be going then."

"Good." She turned towards the back door, before barking: "And I don't want to see you lingering outside my pub again."

△

I headed towards the road, nestled between two thick hedges. *This must lead to the other side of Black Lake,* I thought. It would make sense that he lived here. That's where I'd seen him heading after the procession. *Is this where he watched me?*

Timed his scares? It was about time I confronted him and got some answers.

There was no sign of him now on the long, narrow road. If it wasn't for Bertha, I would have caught up to him by now. I'd been stalled. I took out my phone, wondering if I could phone him. I tapped the phone call icon beneath a deep crack, but nothing happened. I hit it repeatedly, but it would not open. *Stupid smart phones.* It must be only able to receive calls now. I'd have to try some of the houses instead.

The first house was a bungalow hidden behind trees and numerous bales of hay that occupied the garden. All the curtains were drawn, but there was smoke rising from the chimney. I reached the doorstep and knocked. Something shuffled inside. Shadows moved behind the curtains. But no one came to the door. I knocked on the door again. This time, there were no sounds and no movement.

Disappointed, I returned to the road and tried two more bungalows, with no luck.

This was probably where Mick had lived, or Tom and Adam, I thought.

I was getting restless; Brian could live anywhere. Then, as I was turning to head back up the road, I observed a two-storey house at the end of the road. It couldn't have been more than a five-minute walk. It was worth a shot.

I broke into a light jog, passing a couple of farms with sheds packed to the brim with bales. The smell of hay, strong and damp after months of sitting in the cold, filled my nostrils. When I reached the end of the road, I stopped and bent over, hands on my knees, my lungs desperate for air. I hadn't jogged this much in months. Ever since… I couldn't remember. I had never liked the idea of exercising outdoors in the polluted air of London. At least, that was my excuse.

Once my breathing calmed, I continued to the house. It was quiet here. I could just about hear the cars from the village, but the surrounding fields were populated only with sheep – ewes – too fixated on eating grass to notice me approaching.

A car was parked outside the house. The curtains were open, a TV flickering inside. Might this be Brian's house? I'd never seen his car, I realised. I suppose he was close enough to the cottage to walk, if this was indeed where he lived.

I rang the bell. It buzzed loudly. I heard no other sound.

I tried ringing it again, before stepping away.

Seriously?

I looked up and saw a hand pulling a curtain across the top-right window. I realised all the other curtains had been drawn already. These people clearly didn't want any visitors. Perhaps some were mourning their neighbours' deaths. Or maybe they just didn't want to see *me*.

That can't be possible, I thought as I headed back to the road. These locals hardly knew me, other than Brian. Unless word had spread, and they knew who I was. What I'd done.

Had all three been in the same tractor? Surely that was reckless. How did that make me a killer?

I became distracted by something moving in the corner of my eye, in the field at the end of the road. I lowered my glasses and saw a figure heading up a hill in a hat and dark coat, their back to me. The same hat and coat I'd seen the figure wearing behind the procession, and watching me on the edge of Black Lake. The same hat and coat I'd seen Brian wear.

Over the Hill

"Brian!" I shouted, noticing he walked using a stick. Probably a branch for the climb, and to wade his way through the thick bushes and briars that encircled the hill. *"Brian!"* I shouted again. He didn't turn. Where was he going?

I reached the gate that led to the field, only to find it locked with a chain. I climbed over it quickly, afraid that I would lose sight of him. My shoes sunk into the muddy ground, water seeping through and wetting the tips of my socks. I could smell an earthy scent of mud and wet grass. I started to sprint, surprised by my speed. The soft earth squelched beneath me.

I continued running, careful not to slip into the deep, rain-filled cattle tracks, gasping for breath. By the time I reached the foot of the hill, the figure had already disappeared behind it.

I hurried as fast as my legs would allow, elbowing my way through the thorny briars, trying not to get pricked, though that didn't stop my face from being whipped and scratched. The muscles in my legs strained, fighting the sudden pressure I was exerting on them after months of inactivity. By the time I reached the top of the hill, I was barely walking.

I stood as tall as I could, stretching my back, and gazed down at the fields below. There was no sign of Brian.

I'd lost him.

I surveyed the surrounding countryside. Nothing moved, except the tops of the forest trees enclosing Black Lake. Sheep bleated in the distance. I could see the outline of a house, about fifty metres away from the water's edge. Raising my glasses, I realised it was just the ruins of a house: the roof was missing, and stones lay scattered on the ground around it. A dozen black bales sat behind the house, next to the ruins of what looked like had been a shed.

Could that be the house? I wondered. *Wasn't Jim Harrow's house by the lake?*

I watched the house, wondering if Brian had gone inside. But why would he go inside Jim Harrow's ruined house?

I paused, catching my breath, wondering if I should turn back. But I was so close to the ruined house, and Brian was possibly inside. Was it safe to confront him here? Given how isolated I was now, the thought was less appealing. *Who knows what he's up to, what he's capable of?* I thought I was pretty good at understanding people, at least in terms of deciphering my own characters in more than a dozen novels, and still I struggled to get my head around Brian. For all I knew, he could be a stalker psychopath. It was too risky, confronting him out here with nobody around. I could visualise it easily: Brian hitting me over the head with a rock before throwing my body into the lake. It wasn't worth it. It'd be better to return to the car.

Something stopped me. I spotted a couple of children jumping across the wrapped bales of hay, behind the house. Had they been playing there all this time?

There might even be a family nearby. At least there were other people around if confronting Brian didn't go to plan.

I started to descend the hill towards the ruined house. I observed the few windows that remained, boarded up with wooden pallets, and great black holes around them where masonry was missing. I supposed the fire had burned the roof, if this was indeed the Harrows' home.

The children's laughter reached my ears, screaming with delight as they jumped from one bale to the next. I remembered how that felt; the thrill of the leap before landing onto the next bale safely. Rachel and I, as well as other local kids, would break into the farms that had the best-looking bales, and spend the day jumping from one to the other. We weren't loitering outside shops or on street corners, like the kids in London. We spent our days searching for the best bales. Of course there were times when I didn't make it to the next bale and fell into one of the deep crevices, but trying to escape that tight situation was just as thrilling.

I reached the bottom of the hill where I had a better view of the children. The boy, perhaps five or six, was wearing a rather worn suit jacket, too short for his arms, and had a mass of black, wavy hair. The girl appeared even younger. She wore a flowing white dress, the hem a little muddied. I thought I'd seen the girl somewhere before. They were both laughing, completely oblivious to me.

I became aware of a creaking sound beside me. The front door was swaying slowly, barely supported on its rusty hinges.

I made my way towards it, the children's laughter fading in my ears.

I held the door as I stepped inside, in case I might slip. Stones littered the ground, much like outside. I was surprised to see a partial staircase before me, only a pillar and couple of beams still standing beneath an absent first floor. The ground was mostly stone with grass seeping through cracks, and muddy tracks from sheep and other animals – possibly the only visitors now.

"Brian?" I called, moving closer to the remaining stairs. I stopped when I realised I'd stepped on something. I looked down, expecting to see my shoe covered in cow crap, but was surprised to find a brown and battered trilby hat. I got down on my hunkers, picking it up. The edges were smeared with mud, most likely from my shoe.

Brian's hat? I wondered, turning it in my hands.

I heard a cough in the distance. I made my way to the door and peered through the chink: someone was storming down the hill, a tweed cap obscuring their face. He was too short to be Brian. He was bent forward, hands deep in his coat pockets, ploughing through the grass in big black wellington boots. A light mist, which hadn't been there before, had settled on the hill behind him.

I opened the door fully, hoping to get his attention. The man was walking fast towards me – only metres separated us.

"Hello?" I offered with a smile – I didn't want to upset another local.

The man stopped instantly. For a second, I thought I'd seen red, bulbous cheeks, but the colour drained so fast from his face I was convinced I'd imagined it. He stood motionless, his eyes fixed on me. I stood just inside the door, studying him. *He must be a farmer*, I thought. *Checking up on his fields.*

But why didn't he speak?

We continued to stare at each other as the mist drew closer around us. I'd expected him to be angry, encountering a stranger on his land. But he didn't look angry. His face was so still, it was hard to find any expression there at all. His eyes never blinked.

What was he staring at? Couldn't he see me?

I whipped around, expecting to find someone, or something, standing behind me. Nobody was there. I turned back to the farmer. His eyes were definitely fixed on me.

"Hello?" I said again, broadening my smile.

His bottom lip quivered slightly, and I couldn't tell if it was from the cold or if he was trying to speak.

"Y-you," he managed to stutter. He stretched his arm in my direction. "You, you…"

I waited for him to finish his sentence, but he took a step backwards, his eyes still focused on me.

"You, you, you're a ghost," he said.

I think my mouth fell open then, and so did his.

"Look," I managed to say, taking a step towards him.

"Stay back!" he shouted.

I stopped, surprised.

He stumbled backwards, up the misty hill, never taking his eyes off me. I could only stand and stare, too shaken to move or speak.

What was happening?

Thoughts ran through my head as I watched the farmer stumbling backwards up the hill. Had he seen a ghost? Did he think *I* was a ghost?

His frozen expression had imprinted itself on my brain – I still can't get it out of my head now. I'd never seen colour drain so fast from a face before. And his grey eyes: unblinking, unwavering. He had looked genuinely terrified, as if he truly had seen a ghost.

But how could he believe *I* was a ghost?

I realised I was still holding the old hat, long after the farmer had disappeared over the hill. Could he have thought *I* was Jim Harrow?

I dropped the hat, wiping my hands on my jeans as if they were contaminated. It was just a hat, I told myself. It probably belonged to the farmer. But that didn't explain why he was absolutely terrified.

I headed outside, wondering if the children were still playing on the bales. I began to fear the mist would turn to a thick fog, and I wouldn't be able to find my way back onto the road; such were the perils of the countryside. But when I turned the corner, there weren't any children playing on the bales. They were both gone.

Deciding they were the farmer's children, and he'd come to get them, I made my way up the hill. My legs were still tired, and my progress was slow. My face stung from the scratches.

At last, I hopped over the old gate. I half-wished a car would come along and carry me the rest of the way. But there weren't any cars and, after having had no luck at these houses, I doubted anyone would offer me a lift. I could imagine that farmer sitting inside Castlestrange Lodge now, knocking back something strong, a crowd gathering around him as he told everyone he'd just seen a ghost. Not any old ghost, but the ghost of Jim Harrow.

The return of Jim Harrow. Another reason for them to loathe me even more.

Perhaps they all believed it was the ghost of Jim Harrow who'd killed Mick and his nephews. That's what Bertha seemed to imply. And now she thought everyone else in her pub was in danger. Whatever the case, it was time for me to leave this place. I didn't belong here. Perhaps I never belonged here, and never would again.

IX

Anne, 1939

Letter from Anne Harrow to Maud Kavanagh

Fairy Hill
30th August 1939

Dear Maud,

The fairy doctor came to visit this morning. A complete and utter waste of time, to be honest. Still, let me tell you all about it so you can understand why I won't be running to fetch another one any time soon.

Jim said the fairy doctor had requested we light a fire in the hearth and bring Brendan downstairs to lay beside it. Jim had told me nothing, only that he is the best fairy doctor in the county. To be honest, I'd been expecting it to be an old woman, but indeed there was a man making his way down the hill in a long white shirt, his bald head and white beard glinting in the morning sun. I called to Jim that the fairy doctor was coming, and he headed upstairs. Not a second later there was a knock on the door. I answered, not sure how to greet a fairy doctor man, but as soon as I opened the door, he hurried past me, saying there was a bad history of human-fairy relations around the place, and we were all in great peril. Not the greeting I was expecting, but I suppose I've never met such folk before.

The man asked for Brendan, and I told him Jim had gone upstairs to fetch him. I offered him tea, but he shook his head and unbuckled his large briefcase, ready to get to work. He had a bony face and a long, thin nose. He was also very stooped, and I noticed a large hump on his upper back as he rummaged inside his briefcase.

I had a quick peek at what was inside: coloured bottles, some transparent, and bits of bushes and wild flowers. It was such a basic assortment I wondered if he was a charlatan. My stomach churned, and I felt silly not to have done some research on fairy doctors beforehand. But who can I turn to for fairy research other than you?

The loud clang of Jim's boot on the stairs behind me made me jump. Brendan's limp body hung in his arms, his skin deathly pale. As he carried him down the stairs, the fairy doctor scattered what looked like herbs onto the fire. I could smell rosemary, but there was something foul too. When the fairy doctor was done, Jim placed Brendan on the rug before the fire and I grabbed a couple of pillows to place underneath his head. The child's skin was hot and clammy to touch; I couldn't fathom how a roasting fire could help his condition. The fragrances were overpowering. It was so stifling that I was relieved when the fairy doctor told us to leave the room, saying no one could bear witness to the mystery of his power. As Jim and I headed upstairs, I glanced behind me to see the man hunched over Brendan, mixing herbs and whispering what sounded like a prayer.

We sat upstairs in the bedroom for what felt like hours. There were times I stood up to go have a peek, but Jim grabbed my arm and warned I might break the fairy doctor's spell. He must know a great deal about these fairy doctors that he's not telling me. I had to sit there struggling with all sorts of thoughts of what he was doing to Brendan. It was an agonising wait, and I was flooded with relief when I heard him making his way up the stairs.

Jim and I stood to meet him, but the expression on his wizened face did not suggest good news. In fact, he was trembling, grasping his briefcase tight.

"He's been struck with a bad case of the fairy stroke," he pronounced. "I suspect out of the fairy's anger for what has happened on this land."

I turned to Jim, whose eyes had narrowed. There was a knowing look on his face. I didn't know what to say, or how to react. I didn't know what this meant.

"What does that mean, a fairy stroke?" I finally asked. "And what do you mean, 'on this land'?"

"The fairy stroke is quite common in children," the fairy doctor explained. "Particularly handsome children. If left too long untreated, and too long unprotected, the child's body and spirit will gradually wane, until the fairies can finally take his soul."

"Take his soul?" I repeated. The fairy doctor nodded, his hands squeezing the strap of his briefcase. "But why?"

"That's all the fairies ever want, Mrs Harrow. A handsome child. But their exact purpose for Brendan... that can only be known to the fairies. Some keep them as their own children, whilst others offer them to satisfy the Evil One."

"The Devil?" I whispered.

"That's enough now," Jim interrupted, his voice low and grave. "Just tell us how he can be helped."

"I'm afraid it may take a very long time to reverse the fairy's spell," the fairy doctor lamented. "At present, your son is at the height of risk from being taken. He is very weak and extremely susceptible. Therefore, you must protect him at all costs from any more fairy exposure. That means keeping him by the fire. A turf fire is best. I also advise he takes a spoonful of this daily," he added, handing

over a bottle of dark, brown liquid from his case, the colour of bog water.

"What is it?" I asked, inspecting the bottle in my hands.

"The strongest mixture of herbs for a child in this late stage of the spell," he answered. "This should help him improve. But be patient. It will take a long time to undo the damage done. But, as I said, Mrs Harrow, your child is still at great risk, even if he does improve. The best thing I would advise in this situation is to take your son away from here. In fact, take all your children away. This land is not safe, especially to those most vulnerable."

"Why not?" I demanded. Jim shuffled beside me. "What is it about this land?"

I saw the fairy doctor's eyes flick to my husband. I know it wasn't fair, keeping me in the dark. Neither of them uttered a word. A low moan sounded from below. I hurried down the stairs and saw Brendan slowly roll away from the fire and onto the stone floor. He must have been roasting down there.

"I will leave you now," the fairy doctor said as I made my way to Brendan. "But take my counsel wisely."

I knelt beside Brendan, taking his head in my hands. His skin was like hot iron, and his clothes were drenched. Even the rug beneath him was damp. Strange marks had been drawn across his forehead, like ash or soot from the fire.

"He's overheated," I called. I turned to find Jim still standing on the stairs, his eyes fixed on our son. There was no sign of the fairy doctor; I hadn't even heard him leave. "He needs cooling," I said. "And then to see the doctor."

But your brother didn't move; it was like he was transfixed.

"Grab a damp cloth from the kitchen, Jim," I said. "Jim! We need to cool him down. Jim!"

His face had grown dark, except for the reflection of the red fire in his eyes. The house, too, seemed to have filled with shadow, as if a storm was brewing outside. Jim's eyes beamed red from the shadows. Why wasn't he moving? Why wasn't he helping his son?

The fire crackled beside me, lighting Jim's face. I wasn't sure if he was watching me or Brendan. He looked distant. And though he had once been a strong and well-built man, he was now unusually thin. His face had become sharp and angular, his cheeks sunken. He was always well-kept – not as groomed as some of the other village men, but he always managed to scrub up. Now his face looked unclean and unshaven, stubbly, and his clothes worn and shabby. Perhaps it had been my fault for not noticing? Perhaps I've been focusing so much on Brendan that I haven't even noticed my husband has also been ill. I should have been supporting him too. How can I be failing both my children and my husband? I will try better, Maud, I will try.

We didn't manage to take Brendan to the doctor. Your brother went to fetch his hat and coat and headed out, back to the inn, I suppose. I couldn't carry Brendan all the way to the village myself. Instead, I took him back upstairs and settled him in a cold bath to cool him. Still, I'm so vexed with the whole event, you would not believe. I cannot believe Jim invited some charlatan into our house to make up potions and incant charms, who then had the nerve to say our son's soul could be taken to 'the Evil One'. He must not be of sound mind. And what is all this nonsense about the land? Land is land, it doesn't have feelings. How can land be a threat to Brendan?

That's enough of fairy spells and fairy doctors for now. Maybe I'll ask the doctor in the village to visit him here. I will keep an eye on your brother, but it is difficult when he spends much of his time at the inn. I am not sure why he spends the whole day there. I can only assume it must be the stress of an ailing son and a failing wife.

If there is something better you can suggest for Brendan, please do.

But please be aware I will be having no more of this fairy nonsense from now on.

God bless!

Anne

X

Rick, 2019

The Photograph

I sat in the car outside a couple of internet cafés before deciding they were too busy. I couldn't risk being seen in my haggard state, my face covered in scratches. Then, I remembered the town library, next to the ruins of an ancient abbey. That should be quiet, surely, in the middle of the day?

As hoped, the library was quiet: if there were any visitors, they were hidden behind shelves or desktop computers. I suspected I'd need some sort of code to log into one of the computers, so I summoned the energy to enquire at the front desk.

"You're not Rick Rooney, by any chance?" the librarian asked as he handed me a slip of paper with my guest credentials. I paused, surprised to be addressed by my author name, before remembering I was in a library.

"Yes," I said, taking the paper.

The librarian seemed surprised. I wondered if they had many authors visit the library.

"Can you sign a book?" he asked, before ducking under the desk.

"Sure." I hadn't expected to be signing autographs. Cynically, I hadn't even thought about having fans, or even readers, in my hometown. The librarian reappeared from under the desk, pulling a book from his backpack. My book: *The Haunting of Elm Manor,* with its generic stock image of a dilapidated old house above the title. Looking at the cover made me feel queasy: I didn't like the image, and I absolutely detested the title. "Marketing said your working title lacked keywords," Pierce had commented dryly when he returned the final draft with the 'new and improved' title. "Best listen to the experts. It should be search-engine-optimised now."

The title read like something a stupid bot had automatically generated, not a marketing team. I would have just settled with *The Elm Haunting* as a compromise, but they never consulted me once about it.

I opened my book and signed the title page.

"Thanks," the librarian said as I slid the book back to him. I didn't want to look at it any longer. I thought that was the end of this exchange, but then he asked, "Would you mind getting in my selfie?"

My stomach plummeted. I hated having my picture taken, and I especially hated disappointing fans. "I'm sorry," I responded, attempting a smile. "I don't do photos."

"That's okay." He examined my face. Eyeing my scratches. He frowned, disappointed at seeing me in the flesh, no doubt. Then again, authors weren't traditionally known to be front-page models.

"I've got to do some, um, research," I said.

"Of course." The young man smiled, cradling my book in his hands. I knew I had some young readers, but I didn't expect them to love my work. "You should come back," he suggested. "When you're not so busy."

I experienced a pang of guilt for not visiting my home library more, especially as I had readers here. Well, one confirmed reader.

"I'd like that," I said.

I settled myself in a dark corner and entered the login details. The first thing I did was check my emails. I'd amassed over a hundred emails in less than a week, mainly requests for endorsements for debut authors, spammy book promotion services and, of course, emails from Pierce. Ignoring them, I did a quick inbox search for 'Brian' and opened each of the trail of emails that appeared. They were all via the holiday website and didn't include a personal email address. He'd signed all the emails with 'Brian.'

I sighed and leant back in the chair. I wasn't a detective. Sure, I could carry out extensive research in a short amount of time, but I'd never investigated a living person before. Shaking my head, I sat up and decided to look into Jim Harrow instead, see if anything existed online about him, his suicide and the fire that destroyed his home and killed his family.

Loads of recent news articles and businessperson pages appeared, all too recent to be about someone from the early twentieth century. What year had Brian said the fire had been? Hadn't he said the spirit board came to the pub in the 1930s? But the fire wasn't until…

"Thirty-nine," I murmured, looking around to see if anyone had heard before realising it was just me and the librarian. I turned back to the computer and quickly typed *Jim Harrow fire 1939.*

Nothing of interest appeared, only random news articles and pieces about the fires of London. I was wasting my time, clicking dozens of links. And I really ought to be booking accommodation, or a flight back to London if it was still possible that day.

I looked over at the young librarian, who seemed to be engrossed in a book. What if the library had something about the fire, something from long before the internet? I logged out of the computer, got to my feet and headed back to the desk.

I cleared my throat, hoping I wouldn't frighten him. Even so, he jumped, then slammed the book shut. It was *The Haunting of Elm Manor*. His face turned red, almost masking his many pimples.

"Sorry to interrupt," I said, "but I was hoping you could help me with something."

He sat up straight. "Of course," he said, pulling his keyboard towards him.

"Not with a book exactly," I elaborated. "I was hoping you could help me with some… research." That would keep it less suspicious. "Do you have any papers or history records from 1939?"

"We should," he said. "Although I think you need to sign something. Let me check." He stood, then darted into a back room. Some minutes later, he returned with a folder. *Old-fashioned*, I thought. "I just need you to add your details and also the time."

Once I'd filled in the required details, he led me down a hall and opened a door at its very end. The room was pleasingly dim. "We've got racks of drawers," he pointed out. "The thirties are all the way in this corner, and I'd expect 1939 to be over there. We're in the process of digitalising all this content, or were in the process." I think he was waiting for me to say something. "Library cuts, you see," he finally said.

"Oh," I responded. I didn't know what else to say. Did he expect me to donate to the library? I could barely cover my share of the rent.

"Let me know when you're finished so I can sign you out," he said.

Once he'd left, I opened the last drawer and flicked through the files. I was already spending too much time investigating Jim Harrow, and I was probably never going to find anything. I didn't want to miss any later flights, if there were any.

It took several minutes for me to realise the papers were categorised by month, which would have been incredibly useful to have known to begin with. I was hoping to see a photo of a fire raging across the front page of a newspaper – surely a house fire killing a whole family would be front-page news? At last, I came across the word *FIRE* in bold, under the month of October. October 31st, no less. Halloween.

The night I played with his board.

I grabbed the newspaper by its edges and pulled it out to read the headline: *BLACK LAKE HORROR: FIRE KILLS FAMILY OF EIGHT.*

There wasn't a photo of a fire on the front page – of course there wouldn't be, I realised, as cameras weren't as prevalent then – but instead a photo of the aftermath. The roof had been burnt off, as expected, but most of the walls were still intact and the windows were deep, black holes. Most unsettling of all was what appeared to be white bags littered on the ground which, on closer inspection, were in the shape of bodies. The article took up most of the front page:

A FAMILY of eight perished when a fire destroyed their home in the early hours this morning outside Castlestrange village. A local farmer, John Brennan, noticed the fire on his way home from the Harrow Inn between the hours of two and three, then raised the alarm. The Harrow family, owners of the popular Harrow Inn, are all believed to have been killed. Of the eight, seven bodies have been removed from the remains, and the Gardai and local firemen are still searching for the eighth body. The family home was badly damaged and remains sealed off as the Gardai and firemen carry out their search and investigation. A spokesman said, "The cause of the fire is not yet known, and the Gardai are keeping an open mind..." *[continued on page 3]*

I flicked to page 3, where there was an extensive interview with the local farmer as well as other onlookers. A large photo in the middle of the page showed the Harrow family, outside their inn. Children stood around their parents: four boys and two girls. Both girls were dressed in dark dresses, their faces and arms pale and freckled, and their hair tied in ponytails. But it was the youngest boy who caught my eye, leaning against his mother. He wore a tight jacket and had dark curly hair, possibly black, much like the boy I'd seen playing on the bales earlier. But they could hardly be the same children!

My eyes were then drawn to the centre of the photo, to Jim Harrow's face. I knew the face. I held the paper closer to the light, hoping my eyes had deceived me. But there he was, sitting amongst his family in a photo allegedly taken in 1938:

Brian.

Brown eyes. Dark brows. A long, straight nose. Thick black hair beneath a trilby hat. Clean shaven. I dropped the newspaper. It wasn't possible. But Bertha had said she'd never heard of a landlord named Brian.

So who owns the cottage, Rick? A ghost can't rent out properties!

Apart from the boy, I realised I'd never seen any of the other children's faces by the river. In fact, I don't even think I'd seen the boy's face properly. The link was too tenuous. They couldn't be the same children. There were loads of children in the countryside who wore old clothes. But that didn't explain Brian. The man in the photo was undoubtedly Brian.

I shook my head, filed the paper away quickly and closed the drawer.

There was only one way to solve this: phone Brian from the library.

I reached into my jacket to retrieve Brian's note with his number. My pocket was empty. I tried the other pocket, but that was empty too.

Shit!

I must have lost it, or left it at the cottage. Closing the door of the room behind me, I returned to the front desk and logged the time in the book before hurrying back to the computer. There must be a contact number somewhere for Brian. Opening my inbox, I scrolled through the thread of emails, but couldn't spot any phone numbers. I clicked on the photo of the cottage at the bottom and searched the property's page. There was only a generic enquiry box. No email addresses or phone numbers.

I needed to phone him, somehow, otherwise I would start to question Brian's very existence. But without a phone number – or indeed a working mobile phone – it wasn't going to be easy. Could I have left his note at the cottage? It was possible, dropping it in my haste to get out of there.

I would have to retrieve it: I couldn't succumb to believing in ghosts – I'd never be able to will myself to write another horror book again. But the only way to retrieve it, and get the truth about Brian, was to return to Black Lake.

It's me, Ricky

I drove through the thickening fog, barely under the speed limit, my foot firm on the pedal. I couldn't relax, or even think about leaving, knowing the truth was just a phone call away.

Black Lake was blanketed in fog. The cottage was completely hidden; I had to use my phone light to guide me in its direction, until the motion-sensor light activated. Clay still carpeted the ground, and bits of pottery were scattered everywhere. I had no intention of cleaning it up, not yet anyway. After extracting the key from under a shard, I pushed the door open and stepped inside. I scanned the floor, only to see a slip of paper beneath my shoe. I crouched to pick it up and unfolded the paper: Brian's note. I must have dropped it on my way out.

Shutting the door against the impending fog, I marched towards the telephone in the hallway, picked up the handset and then dialled the numbers. Nothing happened. I tried again, jabbing the buttons with my finger, my patience running low. Still no sound. Was I dialling it correctly?

Pressing the phone closer to my ear, I realised there was no sound at all. No dial tone. It had been years since I'd used a landline telephone, but I knew there should be some sound.

I got to my knees and checked under the table. The cord was plugged into the wall. I yanked it out and then plugged it in again, but it made no difference. There was still no dial tone.

"Shit!" I howled, throwing the handset against the wall, half-hoping it would smash. All the same, I picked up the handset and settled it back in place.

"Fuck!" I yelled. I was truly running out of patience now, and I didn't want to drive back into town, not in the dense fog. Or worse, back to Castlestrange Lodge.

Excuse me, Bertha, may I use your phone? Don't worry, I won't contact anyone who's dead.

I chuckled, taking the half-empty bottle from the cupboard, and poured myself a small glass. I stared at the wall of fog outside the window. The liquid went down too easy, warming my insides, soothing my nerves. I poured myself another glass.

When the bottle had emptied, I decided to face the fog, take the car into town and find a way to phone Brian. That was the point of fog lights, after all. I'd only had two or three small glasses, and it hadn't gone to my head yet, only warmed my stomach. Besides, I had no other option.

Stop, Rick, that's the alcohol talking. Stay put, it'd be safer.

Stay put? And wait for Brian to show up again? What if I'm asleep when he comes? What would he do to me then?

I chucked the empty bottle in the bin, grabbed Brian's raincoat and marched to the door.

All was quiet outside. The fog had grown denser. I held my phone out before me, but it did little in the way of providing light, even with the motion-sensor light shining behind me. Needless to say, there was no sign of the car, or the lake, due to the fog.

I closed the door firmly behind me. Driving back into town was out of the question. I hung up Brian's raincoat and slumped into a chair at the kitchen table. My head dropped into my hands; the whole ordeal had taken a considerable amount of energy from me. But I couldn't bring myself to get up, nor did I want to sleep. I sat there for some time, unable to move. The cottage was completely silent. When I felt like I was falling into a slumber, a cold draft passed the nape of my neck, keeping me awake. I tried to ignore it; I guessed it was coming from the fireplace. But the cold breeze continued, coming from somewhere behind me. I turned my neck to see the top kitchen window slightly ajar. And below, sitting upon the worktop next to the sink, was a bottle of brandy.

I rubbed my eyes and looked again, but the bottle was still there, full and very, very real. Clutching both sides of the table, I pulled myself to my feet and made my way to the window, pushing it closed.

How had that opened? Was it slightly open all this time?

I reached for the bottle, letting my fingers slide down the cold, smooth glass. It looked like the bottle I'd purchased for Brian from the shop, but I had no recollection of taking it inside. Unless Brian, if he really was Brian, had brought another bottle while I was out and opened the window to let in some fresh air. Whatever the case, someone had brought a new bottle, and having a drink couldn't do me any more harm, not after that day.

I tore off the seal and poured myself a full glass, before carrying the bottle and glass to the table.

I sat back in the chair, enjoying the warm sweetness on my lips, rolling the glass in my hand. Hours passed, and at some point, during the quiet night, I finally dozed off. I know I did, because I was crudely woken by a high-pitched ring. It took me some time to register what it was, as I slowly returned to consciousness. On and on it rang, echoing through the cottage

– the unbelievable but unmistakable sound of a telephone.

I jumped from the chair, relieved to know it was working again. Perhaps I could make some calls of my own, the first being to Brian. Before it could ring off, I grabbed the handset and pressed it to my ear. I could hear a low crackle on the other end.

"Hello?" I asked. The crackling continued. I thought I heard breathing. "Hello?" I repeated.

"Ricky?" a voice said. I knew that voice, but I hadn't heard it in years.

"Who is this?" I asked, clenching the handset, unwilling to believe this was happening.

"It's me, Ricky." Then there was warm laughter. "It's Dad."

I froze. *It can't be him*, I thought. My grip tightened around the handset, so tight it might have snapped. Yet, although I was frozen to the spot, petrified, I wanted to hear more. I had to know who this person was.

"Who is this?" I asked again, surprised by my terseness. I wanted to scare him; I had had enough of being messed around with. "Is this you, Brian? Look, you're not scaring me, so you might as well tell me who you are."

"I've told you, my lad."

My lad. That numbed me completely. I couldn't move. I could only listen.

"I've been waiting, son."

"Dad?" I asked, hearing a wobble in my voice. I had to lean against the wall; my legs were trembling. I felt warm tears running down my face. I hadn't heard his voice in years, not since that last phone call before their crash. They'd always called me weekly, back then. Now, it only seemed natural he'd be calling. It's what he'd always done. "Is it you?"

"It is me, Ricky," the voice laughed.

I broke down into in a sobbing mess. He continued to laugh as I cried.

"Dad," I croaked. Tears poured from my eyes. It *was* him. It was definitely him.

"I've been waiting for you," my father said. "I was wondering when you'd come home."

"I'm home, Dad," I managed to say. I patted my pockets for a tissue to blow my nose. "I'm here. I was planning to visit you and Mum at the graveyard. Where are you? How are you calling?"

"We've been waiting to see you," he said. "Your mother and I. She's here. We're all here. We just want to see you."

"Of course," I said, as if it was the most natural request in the world.

"Just let us in, Ricky," he said. "We just want to see you."

"How?" I asked.

"Open the door," the voice said. "That's all you need to do."

"Which door?" I asked, wondering if he was speaking metaphorically or literally. Did he mean open the door to the dead? To another world? The other side?

He laughed. "The front door, ya eejit."

"Okay, Dad," I responded. This was it. I was finally going to see my parents. Whether it was the alcohol, or the absolute credibility of my father's voice, I was completely convinced. I also desperately wanted to believe it was him. "Wait there."

"Your mother and I will be waiting."

I couldn't help but smile.

I left the phone off the hook as I crossed to the door. I paused and gazed out the living room window, half-expecting to see both of my parents standing outside. But all I saw was the thick fog, now a dirty brown, and pressing against the window.

I pushed down on the door handle. Fog seeped through the crack and swirled around my shoes. I peered out through the gap, ears pricked. But like before, all I could see was the fog. I couldn't even see the ground before me, let alone any people. "Hello?" I called, but there was no answer. Everything was quiet.

Confused, I stepped back and watched the fog seep into the front room. I turned and headed back to the phone, placing the handset to my ear. Instead of a crackling sound, I heard heavy panting, as if my father was gasping for breath, gasping for his life. But Dad had always been an active man, right up the crash. He was never out of breath.

"Dad?" I asked.

The breathing stopped. He cleared his throat. "Relax, Rick," the voice croaked, followed by another gasp for breath. But it wasn't my Dad's voice. Instead, it was low, throaty. Raspy. I wanted to shout down the phone, but my lips wouldn't move. My body grew numb again, so that I could only listen.

The voice started to gurgle. What was he doing? Drinking? Then he started laughing, a deep, guttural laugh, which turned into a hoarse cough. I dropped the handset, and my eyes turned to the wide-open door. The fog was spilling into the cottage fast, circling the coffee table and sofa. But there was nowhere for me to run, except out into the fog.

It must be Brian, I thought. *Brian pulling a prank.*

I slammed the door shut, causing fog to swirl all around me. I looked to the windows, but couldn't see anything except the creamy-brown blanket pressing against the glass. I spun around and headed to the back door, checking to ensure it was locked. I knew all the windows were locked, but that didn't stop me from checking every one of them. But if it was Brian behind this prank, how could I keep him out? He'd entered the cottage before; he could enter again.

At this realisation, I grabbed a stool from underneath the worktop and dragged it to the door, securing it beneath the handle. In the kitchen, I pulled all the drawers open to locate a suitably large knife. I didn't think I'd have to use it, but I felt more protected with it on me. With the stool lodged tight beneath the door handle, and a knife in hand, I switched the lights off and hurried to the bedroom and locked the door. I hauled the chest of drawers from the corner of the room and pushed it against the handle. Then I hit the lights, pulled back the bedsheets and clambered into the bed.

The heavy blanket was a comfort, and I felt safer underneath the covers, like a frightened child hiding from the world. Except I was an adult, and I didn't know who exactly I was hiding from. Still, my heartbeat slowed. A pleasant drowsiness overcame me. I could have easily fallen asleep if I wasn't the subject of a sick prank.

I had no idea what the time was and I couldn't see my watch as it was only analogue; my dad's watch, actually. I felt for my phone and found it in my back pocket. I could just about read the time: it had only gone seven pm.

I couldn't believe I'd fallen for another prank. But how could Brian have impersonated my dad so well? And how could he still be alive, and walking, if he truly was Jim Harrow? That photo had been taken in 1939. Unless he was a descendant who looked exactly like him, pretending to be his ghost. But that didn't explain how he replicated my dad's voice. Whoever had phoned clearly had known my father well enough to have imitated him. Perhaps Brian had known my father, and I simply hadn't recognised him after all these years. But what had I done to deserve this? Why was Brian torturing *me*?

The cottage was incredibly quiet. The only sound was the dull thudding of my heart beneath the duvet. Eventually, I peeped over the covers. The room was completely black. I couldn't even see the window. I took out my phone and shone the light towards it. The fog was still thick outside. I hoped it would clear before the morning; I couldn't spend another night here.

As I was putting away my phone, I heard a dull thump in the distance. I froze, willing my heart to quieten so I could listen properly. I couldn't hear anything more, and I concluded it must have just been my heart thumping.

I was about to crawl out from under the covers when I heard the thump again. It wasn't coming from outside the window; it was coming from outside the bedroom door.

I froze, my head still poking out from beneath the covers. My neck strained due to the odd angle. It must be Brian. He was back. And it must have been him standing at the foot of the bed the other night.

What did he want?

Another thump sounded. Like a heavy book. This time it was close, possibly in the hall. Then the rhythmic sound of footsteps.

Clip, clap.

I gripped the knife handle, tilted the tip away from me. I had to be ready. I had to defend myself.

The footsteps came closer, each louder than the last as they neared my door.

Clip, clap.

He was walking slowly, possibly listening for sounds of

movement. I tried to twist my body to face the door, but stopped when the mattress squeaked. I froze again, listening. However, he didn't quicken his pace. The footsteps came slow and steady.

Clip, clap.

A floorboard just outside the door creaked. I turned the tip of the knife towards the door, preparing to pounce. I could just about see the frame of the door, despite the darkness. My hands were shaking violently. I had to keep still; I couldn't risk dropping the knife. That would be the end.

I kept my eyes fixed on the door, waiting. I couldn't hear any more footsteps. He must be standing directly outside.

I saw the door handle move downwards, accompanied by a slow creaking sound. He was coming in. He'd be inside the room in seconds.

The door began to shake. He was pushing it inwards, against the heavy chest of drawers. I'd almost forgotten I'd placed it there. He shook the door harder and harder, trying to dislodge it completely.

"Please," I found myself whispering, beneath the chaos.

The bashing only grew louder and louder. The door was almost off its hinges and the chest of drawers rocked on its legs. The sound became unbearable.

"Please," I cried, shutting my eyes and pressing my hands against my ears. The knife dropped to the floor, but I didn't care. I had to block out this nightmare, even if it killed me.

Now something hard was hammering against the door. It wasn't the sound of a hand; perhaps it was a stool from the kitchen.

"Go away!" I shouted.

The hammering continued. They wouldn't give up. They'd

get in somehow. "Leave me alone!"

My choking sobs blocked the deafening sounds from outside. It was a relief to find myself crying, actually. I'd rather die hearing myself cry than listening to those dreadful banging noises.

I curled up into a tight ball underneath the covers, tears flowing freely. I can't tell you how long I cried for but at some point I stopped, and so too had the pounding against my door. Eventually, I peered out from beneath the covers to find it was still dark outside. The chest of drawers was still intact, but the door was ajar.

After some minutes of straining my eyes and ears, I felt around on the floor for the knife and gripped its handle. Then I let my body slip from the bed and I got to my feet.

I peered through the chink. The hallway was empty. I placed my ear to the gap but couldn't hear a thing. Feeling reassured, I pushed my shoulder against the chest of drawers and moved it out of the way. I pushed the door open.

There was no movement in the kitchen or living room. The brandy sat open on the table. There was only the stool between me and the front door now, wedged underneath the handle. Running might be the safest option; if someone was still inside the cottage, they might have less chance of catching me if I was quick. With the knife held out in front of me, I dashed down the hall to the front door, kicking the stool aside. I swung the door open and ran.

The fog pressed down on me, becoming heavier and heavier with each step, thin strands sticking to my skin. It weighed on my shoulders, slowing me down. It tightened my chest, squeezing the air from my lungs. I gasped for breath, desperate to see any sign of the car, or anything at all.

Suddenly, I remembered the car keys. I pulled them from my pocket and pressed the button. A dull beep sounded from behind me. I turned and ran in the direction of the cottage – at least, I thought that was where I was heading – pressing the key fob button repeatedly. The beeping grew louder, but I still couldn't discern the shape of a car.

Then I saw something that made me halt: two white faces staring up at me, a boy and a girl, their eyes wide and blood red. I backed away from them, and found my shoe had snagged in something soft, like a blanket. But my eyes stayed fixed on their two small faces, staring out of the fog, and before I knew it, I was falling backwards into ice-cold water.

The shock made me shriek. Adrenaline coursed through my body, and I rolled onto my front, submerging both arms into the water. Something strong was pushing me down. Though the lake was shallow here, I was unable to rise above it. I was sure someone or something was trying to drown me. I crawled onwards, submerged in the icy water, my hands grasping rocks and gravel, my wet clothes dragging me down.

I continued crawling around the edge of the lake, unsure where I was going, until finally I was able to clamber to my feet. As I ran from the water, I realised the great weight had lifted, and I found myself climbing over a muddy trench. I felt my shoes sinking into the soft floor of the forest.

I'm not sure what happened after that; it's all a bit of a blur. The next thing I remember is pounding my fists on a door. I recall being numbingly cold. I kept pounding, my hands raw. Then the door fell way and I dropped into somebody's arms as a voice shouted, "Good God!"

I don't remember anything after that.

XI

Anne, 1939

Letter from Anne Harrow to Maud Kavanagh

Fairy Hill
30th October 1939

Dear Maud,

Thank you for your letter. I cannot express enough how disappointed I am that you persist with these nonsensical warnings. Have I not told you, in detail, what a failure that charlatan was? And haven't I told you that, despite how much I've heeded you, your brother and that charlatan, that there has been no improvement in poor Brendan's condition? Now you tell me that the greatest threat to Brendan at present is the month of November? And not just November, but November Eve? What is this?

You write, "It would be bad for Brendan to be out on November Eve with the other children. Keep all your children inside. If you or Jim are out on that night, and you hear footsteps on the road, do not turn around. It's the dead who are walking, and their glance will kill you." Where do you learn this drivel? And what's this? "It is even worse to be out in late November, when the fairies are at their most powerful, and their most determined. You will hear their revelry on the hills as the month passes, hear their music get louder, their dancing wilder and their laughter madder. Do not let

Brendan near them. Do not let Brendan out of your sight or he will be taken."

Brendan can barely lift a finger, never mind go dancing with the fairies! He has never been so bad. I fear this is the end for him. It's the worst I've seen him and I'm afraid he may not last another week. That's the truth. Now, if there is some miracle cure you can suggest, I am ready to hear it, although I suppose it's too late.

I've been taking Brendan to see the doctor. I had to do something. It was only time. It wasn't difficult carrying a child who is now as light as a feather into the village. Jim doesn't know, of course. He's been spending more and more time at the inn, late into the night, and doesn't get back until the early morning. There's something chilling I have to tell you, Maud. Something frightening, which may even explain Jim's odd behaviour. They may be only rumours, but they would explain everything. But let me tell you what the doctor said first.

Doctor O'Shea says the child is 'delicate' and that there are more and more cases of TB being reported across the country, but he is surprised Brendan has endured the illness for so long. He said there are reports of entire families succumbing to TB in the county, and that it won't be long until we see cases in the village. He suspects Brendan may be the first. And the treatment? None. It is too late now for Brendan to undergo surgery in his very feeble condition.

Maud, it's everything I feared. I've left it far too late. Too late, because I've been messing around scattering primroses around the house, making fires and calling upon fairy doctors. Doctor O'Shea advised the best I can do is keep Brendan away from the rest of the family and not to bring him into the practice again. Now do you understand why Brendan won't even have a chance of being taken by the fairies next month?

And, to top it all off, there are these rumours in the school about

Jim, and God knows where else. Both Fearghus and Fionn came home from school one afternoon, shouting some strange word and saying they wanted to play a game with Jim. They're calling him the Wee-. I'm afraid to even write it here. All I will say is it's to do with some sort of spirit board. I don't want to be connected to those things. And now the whole school seems to want to play with Jim and his board. Who knows, maybe even some of the older children already have.

Oh Maud, we're going to be the talk of the whole village. The alcoholic innkeeper messing with ghosts. It's that board that's been driving him silly, giving him notions about protecting his son from fairies. That and the alcohol, no doubt. I'm not saying he really is an alcoholic – I wouldn't know, I hardly see him. But that's how the village will speak of him. I know it. It's not just the alcohol; it's these notions. There's nothing worse than a man with notions.

And now he has a new one. He said it was the fairy doctor who told him, but it could be an idea he's picked up from that board. Jim says what Brendan needs is a big fire. He said we need to build a turf fire around Brendan's bed so that the fairies don't harm him. It sounds risky enough to me, especially considering how Brendan fared next to the great fire we prepared for the fairy doctor. Not to mention the mess it would make and the danger it would pose. I suppose you've heard of this before? I'll have to try to talk Jim out of it when he gets home tonight, or before he heads to work in the morning.

I will keep you informed about Brendan's health, although I can't see it improving from here. I might have one child less, next time I write to you. It's awful to think about, Maud, but I am lucky to have him. Such a handsome child. I pray if he goes that he will be a little prince in the next life. A happier, stronger and healthier little prince. That's all I can hope for now, or some miracle from God.

Pray for Brendan.
God bless you.
Love,
Anne

XII

Rick, 2019

The Visitor

The man in the hat came to visit me every night. Whenever I woke, I'd find him standing at the foot of the bed, always facing me. I never saw his face, only his hat and long, dark trench coat. A heavy-looking thing, hanging from narrow shoulders. I wondered if it was brown and the whole thing was just sopping wet. The room always smelt damp.

Each night he would raise an arm, always his right arm, as if it was automatic. Something he couldn't control. After a long time standing still, his arm would rise slowly, making me jump, or twitch. Then, he'd pour a liquid all over the floor before dropping the canister, his arm still raised. But he wouldn't light the match. It was like he was teasing me. Tormenting me. He knew, and I knew, what he meant to do. This was his way of drawing out the inevitable. And every night, just when I thought the room would be engulfed in flames, his arm would drop and I'd fall back into my pillow, back into the darkness I thought I had escaped.

It was after several nights I realised this action concurred at a specific time on a clock beside me: 02:20. At 02:20, he would raise his arm, and it would stay raised and motionless for minutes, sometimes an hour. Each time I was transfixed. Waiting. Begging for him to light the match. Anything to end this torment.

Some nights I woke to the sounds of footsteps. Sometimes I woke to the stale stench of alcohol mixed with the dampness. Most nights I woke up crying. And every night he was there. Always standing. Always still. I would try and force myself back to sleep, but I had to watch. This could be the night, I'd tell myself. When 02:20 comes. The night he ends it all.

I would feel nauseous. I seemed to be sweating non-stop, even though my skin was cold to the touch. I began to wake with a heavy lump in my stomach that rose to my chest, and I'd force myself to sit up in case I vomited. But nothing came. The heaviness simply sank back into the pit of my stomach where it dwelt and I'd have to sit with the feeling, hoping the vomit would rise and choke me to death.

When I wasn't awake, I was tortured by strange dreams and wild hallucinations that were so vivid I believed they were real. I could see every word in the news article about the Harrow fire I'd come across that day in the library, as if I held the pages before me. I saw every face in the photo, clearer now than ever, their eyes moving, their mouths curling, as if they were real, living people. I slept terribly due to these images whirling about my head, my entire body was covered in a sheet of cold sweat. Sometimes watching the man standing at the foot of my bed was more bearable than falling asleep.

Then, one day, I woke up and he wasn't there. Instead there was a pale, dim light to my right, struggling to shine through what looked like thick, heavy curtains. Even though it was still dark, the weak light made my eyes sting. My head ached. The clock read 11:30. There was a tray beside me with a cup of tea and dry toast. I sat up and reached for the cup, suddenly realising how dry my mouth was. I gulped the cold tea down.

I couldn't face the toast due to the lump still sitting in my stomach.

After draining the cup, I slid my legs out of the bed and sat up. My head was throbbing, spinning. I waited for it to calm before sliding my feet into the pair of slippers on the floor. I crossed to the window, my legs shaking slightly, before pulling back the heavy curtain.

The glass was wet. Though I could barely see through the misty glass, All I could discern were drops of rain falling from tree branches above me.

Somehow, I managed to drag myself to the door. It creaked as I pulled its handle. There was an unfamiliar staircase before me. It was dark; I didn't know where it would lead. Curious, I gripped the handrail and headed down, careful not to slip on the wooden stairs. It was then I realised how weak I was. My arms were already hurting. My legs wanted to give up. Maybe I was still too exhausted to venture any further than the room. I was probably better off in bed.

"Mr Mulrooney?" came a voice from down the stairs. A sturdy figure appeared at the foot of the stairs, short black hair framing a red face: Bertha. "You shouldn't be up," she said as I took another step.

My knee buckled and my slipper went flying. I gripped the handrail, but I was too weak to hold my weight. I fell back, crashing onto my spine, before sliding down steps and into Bertha's arms.

We climbed the stairs together. Once upstairs, she helped me back into bed. Then she left me, closing the door quietly.

My lower back ached, my head spun, and the room darkened again.

△

The next time I woke up, the curtains to my right were fully open. The light was brighter. Too bright. It looked like there was frost outside. I spotted my prescription sunglasses, hat and gloves neatly laid out on the bedside table, next to a tray with tea and toast.

This time the tea was steaming. I could just about stomach the toast. I realised I hadn't endured any nightmares or hallucinations during the night, nor could I recall any visitations. While I was lost in my thoughts, there was a knock on the door. I tried to move my lips. "Yes," I croaked eventually. My voice sounded strange. Tired. Old. The door opened and Bertha's red face poked through the gap.

"Bertha?"

"Morning," she said, her eyes darting from me to the tray. "You must be famished. I can fetch you some more if you want."

"No," I said hurriedly, fearful that the lump in my stomach would return. "Maybe later."

"Alright." She took the tray. "You have a visitor downstairs. They've been waiting a long time to see you, and take you out of here I hope!"

I nodded, too tired to ask who had come, or why she'd taken me in. As I listened to her pounding footsteps on the stairs, I wondered who'd come to visit me. Had Rachel flown all this way to see me? Nobody else knew I was here, and I sincerely doubted my editor had come all this way to see me.

I listened to footsteps coming up the stairs. "Just in here," I heard Bertha whisper.

The door creaked again. I looked up to see a familiar figure stepping into the room, taking off his hat. Tweed jacket, purple jumper, striped tie and thick, grey hair. His cheeks were flushed, probably from the cold.

"No," I shouted, as loud as my voice would allow, hoping Bertha would hear.

"It's okay," Brian said soothingly as he approached the bed. His tall frame loomed over me. He sat down on the bed, only inches from my leg. "How are you feeling?" he asked, looking me up and down.

"Please. Leave me alone!"

Bertha's voice came from outside the room: "What's going on?"

"Nothing, everything's alright," Brian called back, his eyes firmly fixed on me. "He's still feverish."

I stared into his dark eyes, wondering if it was him who'd come to visit me every night. "Why haven't you killed me already?" I asked finally.

His eyes widened. "Why in the world would I do that?"

"Why don't you kill me now? Set the room on fire, like you've tried before. Do you have it?" I asked, craning my neck to look for the canister. "Or are you going to come back again tonight?"

"What are you talking about?" His dark eyebrows furrowed. "Why would I do something like that?"

"You tried it before, at the cottage," I stated. "And every night since I've been here."

"There was someone in the cottage?"

"Oh shut—" I began. But I didn't have the energy to argue. I was already exhausted from this exchange.

We sat in silence, his eyes looking at the floor. I waited for him to speak.

"Rick," Brian sighed. "I swear I haven't been entering the

cottage, not without you letting me. But if there was someone there, of course I'll need to get the keys and locks changed. And I suppose I should alert the Guards."

"Then who was coming in?" I demanded. I was surprised to find I still had some energy left. "Who was taking towels, leaving footprints, watching me at night?"

He didn't answer. He just continued to stare at the floor as I shouted: "And then someone had the audacity to phone me, and PRETEND TO BE MY DEAD FATHER!"

He was motionless. I was stunned. It sounded so strange to hear those words aloud; someone *had* been tormenting me. But, studying him now in the daylight, how could I have believed he was dead, or pretending to be Jim Harrow?

"Who are you?" I asked finally.

His eyes raised to look at me. His lip quivered; there was something he hadn't told me; I could see it.

"Are you *him*?" I added, though it sounded so absurd. "Or are you pretending to be Jim Harrow?"

He only continued to stare at me. Maybe he was shocked to be asked such a question. Maybe he thought I was mad.

"I am *not* Jim Harrow," he said quietly, his voice almost a whisper. "I am his grandson."

I sat up against the headboard. The face I'd seen in the old newspaper merged into the face before me. They looked about the same age. They had the same dark eyes. Same thick hair. Although the face in the photo was gaunt, as far as I could recall. Haggard. The face before me had a softer, fuller complexion.

"Brian Harrow," I found myself saying. I'd never asked for his surname. "A relative. I thought so."

"No," he corrected me quickly. "Brian McMahon. I took my late wife's surname. Otherwise, I'm sure I'd have been driven out of here long ago."

"I'm sorry," I said, only now understanding he was a widower. "So you live nearby, then?"

He nodded. "Yes."

"Where?"

"In the village," he replied. "Castlestrange." He inhaled deeply before continuing, "I returned after she passed. I always wanted to retire here. I thought it would be good to reconnect. I was ordained as a priest here, in a monastery nearby. There was a college back then. Long time ago. I was young and… Sorry, I'm rambling now. I moved to England, met Angela and left the priesthood. Became a schoolteacher for a while. But I knew the only way to return, and to live here peacefully, would involve changing my name. So that's what I did, after Angela died."

"But all of Harrow's children died," I stated, remembering the article. "At the library, an old newspaper said all the Harrow children perished in the fire. There were no survivors."

"Ah!" Brian smiled, the soft skin around his eyes creasing. "Some of the children survived, including my mother. They were shipped to family in England before the news could even break. The Gardai thought it best to give the children a chance, and not have their lives plagued by their father's sins."

"They covered it up?" I asked in astonishment.

"Yes, like everything else in this country's history. At least this cover-up was for the best."

"That still doesn't explain who was breaking into the cottage," I said finally.

"No," he agreed.

Could it have been *me*? Did *I* leave the wet tracks, misplaced the towel? It was possible, when I'd taken some things to go fishing, and then tripped over it in the fog. Though I had no recollection of taking a towel with me to go fishing. And who had phoned the cottage, and come to terrorise me? "I don't understand," I sighed.

"And how would they have gotten in?" Brian asked. "There are only your set of keys and mine."

"I doesn't make sense," I said, shaking my head. "I couldn't have imagined it. It was so real. The voice. The footsteps. The banging. It's not something you can just imagine. And then there were the children playing on the bales."

"Children?" he asked.

"Yes, next to Harrow's ruined house. I suppose they were the farmer's children, as they disappeared when he left. But I swear I'd seen them before in Castlestrange, on the riverbank. And then I saw them again," I said, remembering the two ghostly children in the fog. "Next to the lake. Just before coming here."

Brian was silent. Pondering. Slowly, he got to his feet and said, "Rick, do you believe in fairies?"

△

There were others who had seen the fairy children too, Brian explained as we sipped on brandy. (Presumably from downstairs, as I hadn't seen a bottle on him). The fairy children were usually sighted near water: alongside a river or next to the lake. It was common for locals to refer to them as fairy children, and people were warned to stay away from them. There were frequent reports of damage, or burglaries, in the area, and some ascribed this to the fairies. Not just fairies, but fairy children of the Harrows.

"They'd play games with the locals," Brian said. "Just being kids. So, I do believe you. In fact, I think one of them is Jim's own son – Brendan."

"Why the Harrows? And why this area?"

Brian pursed his lips, as if holding back his next words. His eyes were fixed on me. Then he reached inside his jacket and pulled out a bulging envelope.

"This will explain," he said. "They were in the car. I found them while researching my family tree. Took me all the way to Boston, where I came across some things belonging to Jim Harrow's sister, Maud. I found other letters too." He handed the envelope to me. "Apparently, the top one there was never sent. I'm not sure why – perhaps Maud had learned the news of the Harrow fire already. Or Maud didn't want to send it, thinking she was keeping whatever curse she believed in all to herself. Here, take them. These are just scans I'd made. They should shed some light on the events leading up to the fire."

"Take them back to London?" I asked.

"If you like." Brian gave a shy smile. "As I said, they're just scans."

"Thank you," I said. "Will they explain who'd phoned me at the cottage then?"

"I don't think it was fairies, if that's what you're asking," Brian said. "After all, you said it sounded like your father."

"They did, just like him."

"Do you think there's a possibility that it *was* your father?"

"No, it couldn't have been," I explained. "Their voice changed. To be honest, it sounded like someone gurgling water, gasping for their last breath."

"Like drowning?"

"Maybe."

"I'm sorry, Rick," he said, getting to his feet. "I'm not sure who called. I'm guilty of filling your head with stories, so you might have just imagined it."

"It wasn't my father, and I didn't imagine it," I stated. "Someone was messing with me."

"I don't know, Rick," Brian shrugged. "Perhaps someone's not too happy you're here. It took a terrible amount of convincing Bertha to let you stay."

I didn't know anyone so upset that I had returned home to drive me out of the cottage. And I didn't want to think it could have been Jim. Instead of ruminating, I sorted through the letters as Brian took our empty glasses downstairs. There was about a dozen of them, all addressed to Anne Harrow. I had much to read and write about; of that I was certain. But I would need Brian's permission. I respected him, even if I'd considered him the source of my torment only hours ago. He'd been kind and, above all, he'd brought comfort when I needed it most.

"I've been thinking," I began when Brian returned. "It's okay," I reassured him. "It's just I'd like to make some notes, but all my stuff is at the cottage."

"Would you like me to go get it for you?" he asked.

"Actually, I'm not sure if you'd want me to…" I trailed off, wondering how to say it. "I'm not sure if you'd want me to write about all this."

"I see," he said, sitting back down.

"I *am* a writer, after all," I said, and it made me feel shameful to say it to him. I didn't want him to think I'd take advantage of him. "But I don't have to include everything," I added quickly. "Not if you didn't want me to."

"I see," he repeated, his gaze lowering to the floor. His hands clenched his knees, crinkling his trousers. "Would it help to include everything?"

"It might help explain a few things."

"I suppose it won't make much of a difference," he sighed. "People barely know me around here. I've tried to keep a low profile. But, can you at least change my name?"

"Of course," I said. He stood up, turned his back to me, and headed to the door. I wondered if I'd caused a rift. Then, as he opened the door, he asked, "Is there anything else you writers need?"

XIII

Maud, 1939

Letter from Maud Kavanagh to Anne Harrow

Cambridge, Boston
7th November 1939

Dear Anne,

I've just received your letter from October. I am sorry to hear Brendan is so poorly. I am keeping him in my prayers, day and night.

I won't repeat myself about you joining us here in Boston, but I do think what you are going through could have been avoided. Haven't I told you before that there is something not right about that place? Not right at all. I always knew it. I mean, we all knew it, but it wasn't until I got your letter about the fairy doctor's visit that I did some proper research. There was something he said that struck me. And now I have to tell you, Anne. I have to tell you everything, because just like the fairy doctor warned, you, Jim and the children truly are in great peril!

I suppose I will have to start at the beginning. Before I left for America. Before I met Donal. Before I even started at the school. There were three of us then: Jim, the eldest; me; and our little sister, Méabh. This all happened when I was very young. It was a beautiful morning – the first Monday of May. We were out collecting stones by the lake. Jim had gone to school and Méabh and I had little to do at home. I remember we were a bit jealous of our brother, and wanted to go along with him to school. Our mother had just run up to the inn, as our father had forgotten his lunch. She was always popping out at odd hours, though – I think it was the boredom of staying in the house all day.

It was a lovely, crisp morning – a clear blue sky reflected in the still lake water below. A hint of the summer days to come. Had it not been cool we might have gone for a swim. We wandered around the water's edge collecting the prettiest stones, our feet bare and the cold water licking our toes.

The stones were piling high in our arms. Méabh was trailing close behind me, singing some old song under her breath. She was always singing something. She had this soft, beautiful voice.

I was unaware then of the risk of a pretty voice on a young girl. I'm not sure when exactly I could no longer hear her, but when I realised, I turned around and she was gone.

At first I thought she must be hiding, but there was nowhere for her to hide around the lake's edge. It was just mud and stones around the lake, except for the forest on the other side that sat beyond the reeds. And she couldn't have run so quickly up to the house – she was a spritely young thing, but she was still very little. The only thing I could think of was the water, but the surface was still.

I dropped the stones and headed into the water, expecting to find her head bobbing just under the surface, ready to jump up and scare me. But there was no sign of her. Not a strand of her long, blonde hair.

"Méabh?" I called. I was starting to get scared. My hands were shaking as I held up my dress. Eventually, I backed out of the water and turned to the house. I sprinted up the hill, all the time shouting for Méabh. Once I was high enough, I turned around to scan the

lake. There was still no sign of her. "Méabh," I screamed, my voice echoing across the lake and to the trees and back. "MÉABH!"

I rushed back to the house, checking every room, every wardrobe and underneath the beds. She wasn't one to play cruel jokes. She was always so nice, cheery, good-natured. Not like Jim, who relished in scaring his younger sisters. I checked in every bush around the house, and up around the fairy rath, but there wasn't a trace of her. That's when I decided to run to the inn. I remember bumping into my mother along the road.

When Jim came home from school, he didn't join the search. Instead, he followed me around the house, asking me all the questions my parents had already asked. What had I seen? Who had I heard? And, over and over again, who had taken our sister? And what had I done? I told him it wasn't me, I didn't see or hear anything, but I don't think he believed me then. I don't think he's ever fully believed me. He was never the same again after that. He became quiet, very inward. He did fine at school, and had a great head for numbers, but he was just never right again. You know how he is. His moods. That all started after our sister disappeared.

I remember being put to bed early that night. Jim and myself. I prayed all night, begging to wake up next morning and find Méabh had returned. I think our parents stayed out all night searching, because when we woke up, they were sitting at the kitchen table, weary and still dressed. My mother's face was very pale that morning, except for the redness in her eyes.

Jim went back to school soon after. He came home one day and told me the rumours the children were spreading. Rumours that haunted me until I finally left that place behind. Boston being so beautiful may have helped me forget. Anyway, I should tell you what the children were saying, if you haven't heard it already. To be honest, I'd be surprised if you haven't: these stories seem to stick around a place like a bad stench, spoiling it for anyone who arrives. I suspect the children heard it from their parents, or their grandparents. The story is old, and goes back to the very origins of my family.

It has also been documented, I discovered to my surprise, in a collection of Irish folk stories I came across in one of the libraries here in Boston. I've written it down for you here, if you haven't heard it already.

A man from England named Robert Harrow, having plenty of money, bought some land, and chose a beautiful green spot to build a house on, the very land the fairies loved best. The locals warned the Englishman that the land was home to a fairy rath, but he only laughed and thought the neighbours overly superstitious. So he built the house anyway, married a local girl, and made it beautiful to live in.

But the fairies were all the time plotting how they could punish the Englishman for building on their dancing ground. They waited and plotted, waited and plotted, until one day the Englishman cut down a sacred hawthorn bush that had sat upon their fairy rath for centuries. This infuriated the fairies even more.

The Harrows had two beautiful boys and an older girl. After the sacred bush had been severed, the youngest boy began to act queer and had his sleep disturbed. He said the fairies came at night and gathered around his bed, and some sat on his chest, and he could neither breathe nor move. This went on and on for nights, and his eyes developed a strange, wild look, as if he saw nothing near him. And when his father asked him what was ailing him, he said the fairies carried him away to the fairy rath every night, where he danced with them until the morning, when they brought him back and laid him again in his bed.

At last, the Englishman and his wife were at their wits' end from despair, for the child was pining away before their eyes, and they could do nothing to help him. One night he cried out in great agony, "Mother! Father! Send for the priest to take away the fairies, for they are killing me; they are here on my chest, crushing me to death," and his eyes were wild with terror.

The Englishman believed in no fairies, but to soothe the child, he did as he was asked and sent for the priest, who prayed over the child and sprinkled him with holy water. The poor little fellow seemed calmer as the priest prayed, and said the fairies were leaving, and sank into a quiet sleep. But when he woke in the morning, he told his parents that he'd had a beautiful dream in which he was walking in a lovely garden with the angels, and that he would be there before night, for the angels told him they would come for him.

Then his parents watched the sick child all through the night, for they saw the fever was still on him, but hoped a change would come before morning, for he now slept calmly with a smile on his lips. As the clock struck midnight, he awoke and sat up, and when his mother put her arms round him, weeping, he whispered to her, "The angels are here, Mother," and then he sank back into his final sleep.

After this misfortune, the Englishman could never hold up his head again. He ceased to mind his land, and the crops went to ruin and the livestock died and, alas, before the year was over, he drank himself to death. The land passed to his remaining son, who worked hard to make the house an even more beautiful place and to restore the livestock, but the fairies' work was not over. Some years later, his child was also struck down by the fairies' curse. And it wasn't long after the child's passing that the Englishman's son, in mourning, took himself to a local church to pray for forgiveness before hanging a noose from a rafter.

And so the land passed from one son to the next, each generation stricken by the fairies' curse – a warning to all who would arouse the vengeance of the fairies by interfering with their ancient ways, possessions and privileges.

Perhaps you now understand, Anne, why Jim is acting the way he is. And perhaps you now understand why I had to leave, not so much out of weakness or cowardice, but out of fear. I too have carried the burden of our sister's disappearance and our father's loss, but Jim has more to worry about, for the fairies' curse does not end with the child's death or disappearance, but takes each father too. I think this is because each father reminds the fairies of that Englishman who first settled on their land and desecrated their home.

I had always thought Méabh's disappearance and my father's death were related to the fairies that lived around our land. That was, until I read one of your letters, Anne. The fairy doctor let slip something, and I am not sure you registered its significance.

Do you know the rumours about Black Lake? I only became aware after Méabh disappeared. It was another reason to stay away.

Black Lake is bottomless. There is no end. A direct passage to him: yes, the Devil. Black Lake is an entryway to hell, and those fairies are his. They work for him, Anne. I am not going to tell you any more – you have enough to worry about with Brendan and now Jim – but I urge you to stay far away from that lake. Far, far away.

I hope to hear from you soon, Anne, and I hope you heed these warnings. I will of course keep praying for Brendan, and for Jim, though I feel there is little I can do to thwart their fate now.

You mentioned in your last letter about Brendan making a handsome little prince. Funny – it's like how I imagine our Méabh. A darling princess, with her bountiful golden locks, bright blue eyes and white dress. I am sure your Brendan will make a fine little prince in Heaven.

God bless you, Anne, and your family. I pray to God the fairies don't take from you as they have me and Jim.

Love,

Maud

PS Look out for Jim, won't you? I fear how he will handle Brendan's passing.

XIV

Pierce, 2020

Email from Pierce Rowlandson to Julia Crouch

From: pierce rowlandson <pierce.rowlandson@caxtonpublishing.com>
Sent: Wednesday, January 1, 2020 7:01 PM
To: julia.crouch@caxtonpublishing.com
Subject: Rick

Julia,

I finished it. I haven't started the letters yet. I'm thinking of saving them for my flight back to London.

Rick stared out the window the whole time I read it. Didn't move at all. I wonder how much he remembers. How much of Rick is even left?

His eyes were closing by the time I finished, but I couldn't let him sleep. The story doesn't have a satisfying ending, Julia. Not really. It just doesn't have a punch. I told him what he'd written was great. Marvelous. But that I had to leave, and I had to know what happened. He didn't nod. Didn't even blink. His eyes had a glassy sheen. I had to hope he was listening.

"What happened, Rick?" I asked again. Then his eyebrows twitched, as if he was remembering or, indeed, trying *not* to remember. "Please," I begged. "Your readers will want to know." I paused, hesitating, then added, "Rachel needs to know." His eyes widened and his head began to shake left and right. "We've all been wondering, especially Rachel. " I examined the white bandage around his head. "How did you hit your head, Rick?" I leant in closer. "Tell me." His bottom lip started to tremble. He was trying to say something. "Speak," I urged. He shook his head, shutting his eyes. Could he even speak? Would he ever speak again? Whatever the case, he wasn't going to tell me there and then. I glanced at the clock: half-past six. I only had thirty minutes left. I'd have to find another way. I reached into my small messenger bag where I always kept a pen and notepad – a habit I'd kept from my days as a journalist – and pushed them into his quivering hands. "Write it down, then," I insisted. "You're a writer, Rick. Better than anyone else at Caxton's." A boost to his confidence always helped. "Write it down for us. Then we'll be able to help." His eyes lowered to the pen and notepad. His head stopped shaking. "Come on," I said, encouragingly. "Pen in hand, that's it." I wrapped his fingers around the pen. They were shaking, and deathly cold. "Let's start with the date, yes?" I moved his hand to the top of the page. "December, wasn't it?" Together, we pressed the pen against the page, and I was relieved to see him writing *18th December*.

He's still writing. There's only five minutes to go before the nurse comes, but at least we're getting something. It might not be a perfect ending, but I'm sure it'll be better than something any of us would come up with.

I better shut down my laptop soon. I'm certain we've got something to end Rick's story with. Reader's aside, *I* would really like to know what happened on 18th December.

Right, here comes the nurse. I need to shut down. Rick's still writing though. I'll write up a summary of Rick's story as soon as I've read the ending.

Regards,

Pierce

XV

Rick, 2019

Fog and Stone

It was early morning on 18th December when I finished writing this first draft, having stayed up all through the night, eager to finish. It has been almost a month since Brian's revelation, and I wanted to get back to London. Brian had checked in on me a few times, never empty-handed, and again only that morning, as I was sprawled across the desk, half asleep. He asked if there was anything else I'd need.

"The rental would help," I said, handing him the car keys. "If that's okay?" I dreaded to know how much I'd have to pay in excess fees.

After quickly packing my things (Brian had offered to bring them from the cottage earlier), I sat back down at the desk and re-read the story Brian had told me. The only thing I hadn't included were the actual contents of the letters, as I was still considering how I'd incorporate them.

[Note to editor: please change Brian's name]

△

"Is that everything?" Brian asked as I packed my suitcase into the boot.

"Almost," I answered, nodding at my satchel bag.

He closed the boot. "Have you had a chance to read the letters?"

"Yes, a couple of times, actually."

"And what do you make of the fairy doctor's assessment?"

I had in fact read the letters a dozen times over, having not had much else to do during my stay at Castlestrange Lodge with no phone or laptop. And still I wasn't quite sure what the fairy doctor and Maud were alluding to.

"I'm not certain, to be honest," I said. "I'm planning on doing a bit of research when I return to London. There's a lot to take in – fairy raths, fairy curses, fairy servants and now fairy children... Mind you, they're good ingredients for a horror book. But what's not clear is the role the Devil played in this family curse, but an understandable theory coming from someone as religious as Maud."

"Accessed through the board?"

I contemplated this. "Jim seemed to be playing the board to help protect his son, looking for answers." I paused again, thinking. "Unless there was something more malevolent at play. The Devil, perhaps, disguising himself as someone else. Perhaps Jim thought he was speaking to his dead sister, Méabh. I suppose that's how the Devil works. Perhaps the Devil persuaded him to go ahead and light the fire, and in turn kill his whole family. Or he was simply following the Fairy Doctor's advice." I looked up at Brian. "What do you think?"

"I'm not sure," he said simply. "I wouldn't like to think the Devil was at play. I like to think Jim was just trying to find ways to help save his son, break this fairy curse, and that they are all at peace. Anyhow, it's a bit much on a lovely day like this."

I listened to the birds chirping around us. In response to a

Content Warnings

This book contains scenes that include:

- alcohol and drug abuse
- arson and multiple fires
- a reference to a suicide
- a reference to a drowning

The author apologies for any other explicit or triggering content not listed above as best efforts have been made to identify and include anything potentially triggering.

About the Author

NP Cunniffe was born in County Roscommon, Ireland, surrounded by dark forests, fairy hills and deep, mysterious lakes. He won a scholarship to the Winchester Writers' Festival in 2017 and was longlisted for the Bath Novel Award in 2020. When the pandemic hit, he self-published a novelette, *The Wake: An Irish Ghost Story*, in August 2020, selling over 500 copies by the end of that year. He holds an MA in Writing the Modern World from the University of East Anglia (UEA), Norwich.

The Weejee Man is his first published novella.

You can connect with me on:

- https://www.instagram.com/npcunniffe
- https://twitter.com/np_cunniffe
- https://www.facebook.com/npcunniffebooks

Subscribe to my newsletter:

- https://bit.ly/NPCunniffeNewsletter

Also by NP CUNNIFFE

The Wake: An Irish Ghost Story

Oxford student Michael has been summoned to the will reading of his old music teacher in the remote West of Ireland. But not everyone is pleased to see him return... Quietly compelling and deeply chilling, *The Wake* is a haunting story about the inescapable power the dead continue to wield over the living.

HLN MAGAZINE RECOMMENDED SCARY BOOK OCTOBER 2020

"Really **excellent** story. I love the spectral echoes of Joyce's The Dead... I was gripped." -Graham Price, author of *Oscar Wilde and Contemporary Irish Drama*

"EXCELLENT! This **creepy novelette** had some unexpected twists... A **perfect rainy night read**!" -Colleen A. Parkinson, award-winning playwright of *The Injured Child* (Shelly Award) and *Waiting for the Train*

"What a **creepy little novella**! The sense of panic and fear and desperation jumps off the page and infests the reader's mind, seeps into the bones like a cold winter day." -Heather Miller, *Quaint and Curious Volumes*

www.ingramcontent.com/pod-product-compliance
Lightning Source LLC
Chambersburg PA
CBHW030608310726
48979CB00003B/618

* 9 7 8 1 9 1 6 4 5 8 5 3 6 *

burgeoning thought, I asked, "If the Harrow family curse was real, will you be safe?"

His eyes closed as the sunlight spread across his face. "I've survived this long," he said. "If it was real, I'm sure it would have got me already. Besides, I don't have any kids. Only fathers were taken."

"Taken by grief," I suggested.

Brian turned to look at me with a solemn expression. "I'll be sad to see you go."

"You've been great," I told him. "Really. I don't think I'd have recovered fully if it wasn't for you."

"You're very kind." Then he grasped my shoulder firmly and, gazing into my eyes, said, "Look after yourself."

I nodded. Once I got back to London, everything would be alright.

"I'd better be off," I said.

"Of course."

"But you have my email," I reminded him as I opened the car door. "I almost forgot," I added, darting inside the pub to fetch my delivery. He looked puzzled when I returned holding a large box in my arms. "To replace the broken pot."

"Oh." Then he broke into a smile. "Thank you," he said. "That's very kind, Rick. Honestly." His eyes were beginning to water.

"No biggie," I laughed, hoping I hadn't set him off. "I mean, I left the place in a right state."

"Yes." He grinned, wiping the corner of his eye with a tissue.

I wondered if he had many friends out here. It must get lonely, as a widower. Or perhaps he preferred to keep his head down in case anyone made the connection between him and the area's history. Maybe that was why he was friendly with me. I was an outsider, like him.

That was the last time I saw Brian. I wonder now if he will ever get to see some of his ancestors playing among the bales, or by the river, like I did.

△

The sun was still shining when I reached the graveyard. It was considerably colder than the last time I had visited, the air that seeped through the window of the car having lost its autumn sweetness. The view before me was strikingly bleak, the branches stark, robbed of their leaves.

The graveyard was quiet. This time, I'd managed to pick up some flowers: a colourful bouquet including lavender, my mam's favourite. For Dad, I brought nothing, because he'd only complain about the price.

Just as I was getting out of the car, my phone buzzed from the passenger seat. I glanced down. The marred screen read *Rach*. I hadn't answered her calls in weeks, with my writing in full flow at last. Was talking on the phone even acceptable here? Wasn't that disrespectful? Surely she'd understand? After all, she had wanted me to visit my parents. Eventually, the phone stopped buzzing.

The cold morning air brushed my face. I'd almost forgotten how cold it was, sitting in the warm car. I zipped up my jacket, tightened my scarf around my neck and headed to the gate. There was frost on the grass and on the headstones, despite the sun. I closed the gate carefully behind me, thinking that the worlds of the living and the dead ought to be kept apart. I've never been a religious person, or a full believer in anything supernatural, but the events of the past months had made me more open-minded. Besides, I'd never resolved what had happened that last night in the cottage. Brian seemed to suggest I'd imagined it. But there was no denying the children I'd seen by the river, on the bales and in the fog, if they truly were the Harrows. So, with my head bowed and my hands clasped together, I entered the graveyard with respect for all those around me.

I took a sharp right to head in the direction of my parents' graves. A quiet corner. In fact, no car seemed to have passed the graveyard since I'd entered it. I wondered if I could become accustomed to this silence again, after living for so many years in London. If I returned to live here with Rachel, I could go fishing regularly, become one of those solitary birdwatchers, find a house for us. Maybe that would be a happier life for me and Rachel. Perhaps she could request to work remotely, if her company allowed it.

I reached my parents' graves in the corner beneath the cherry blossoms. In the spring, the trees would be in full bloom, providing my parents' final resting place with shade from the sun. Now, only a few petals remained. I noticed the sun was already sinking, and grey clouds were gathering above my head.

I laid the flowers against my mother's headstone and bowed my head. They were the only flowers present; a bright, colourful bunch amongst the cold, wet grey of the graveyard. The headstones were already showing signs of ageing, white patches growing on the stone.

As I stood, I thought I could hear children laughing. Through the trees, I saw a boy and girl playing in the older section of the graveyard, in front of the ruined abbey. They looked like the same boy and girl I'd seen playing on the bales, and standing in the fog.

I peered through the branches for a better view. The boy was wearing the same worn, tweed jacket and brown shorts, despite the almost freezing temperatures. The girl was wearing the same muddied white dress, no jacket, and no coat. I couldn't see their faces as their backs were turned to me as they jumped from grave to grave. *It must be the same children,* I thought. The same children from the letters. The same fairy children Brian had wanted to see.

I moved closer. They appeared absolutely real, however. The girl's long blonde hair was bouncing on her shoulders and her muddied hem flapped around her ankles. Now and then the boy would flick his thick, black hair away from his eyes. If you could see them as clearly as I could in the cold, stark, December light, you would also struggle to believe they were anything but real children. But why were they here? What had brought them to the abbey?

A stone wall separated the old graveyard from the new graveyard. There were no more than one hundred headstones, most of them half-obscured by the long grass or sinking into the earth. I tried to keep my eyes on the children.

"Hello," I called as I trudged through the long grass. The children didn't seem to hear me as they jumped from stone to stone, closer and closer towards the abbey. "Who are you?" I shouted, hoping they'd respond to a direct question.

They didn't respond. Instead, they jumped further and further towards the shadowy doorway of the abbey, as if they were actively ignoring me. And it seemed the crumbling abbey was exactly where their game was leading them. What if they were real? Wasn't a crumbing abbey a dangerous place for children to play?

They ran beneath through the arched doorway and disappeared.

"Hey!" I shouted, quickening my pace despite the long grass and lurking headstones. The mound rose as it neared the doorway. I passed underneath the arch to find myself standing in the roofless, rectangular abbey, a grey, gloomy sky overhead.

I could no longer see the children. There was a black sign inside the doorway. I stopped and read:

During the Elizabethan era the abbey was attacked and all its monks slain. The ruins as they exist are of the 17th-century Church of Ireland. The tower was added in 1790, and the church was destroyed by fire in 1870. Interesting headstones depicting the livelihoods of the deceased are found throughout the ancient graveyard.

I heard laughter from a doorway beneath the old tower. I began to worry the children had decided to climb it. One loosened stone and the whole thing would probably collapse and kill them.

I hurried through the doorway and found myself standing beneath the tower. A dark gloom pervaded. I pocketed my sunglasses. It was hard to believe it was the middle of the afternoon. It was so dark, in fact, that I had to take out my phone, but it did little to lighten the place. The darkness was thick, heavy, and I wondered how the children could even see.

I moved around, casting the light in all directions, but I couldn't see where they had gone. The entrance door was completely boarded up. I pointed my phone upwards, but its light did nothing to penetrate the gloom above me. Anyway, I doubted the children could get up there.

I was about to leave when I heard a giggle from just behind me.

I turned around. There was nobody there, but I discerned small alcoves in each corner. I had assumed they were spaces for statues but, on closer inspection, I realised the alcove to my right was in fact an opening to a curved passage. Coldness rippled through my body. I shuddered, and my phone slipped, though I caught it with my other hand. I couldn't lose my only source of light. The phone light illuminated steps spiralling downwards.

"Are you down there?" I called. There was no response. The passage was where the coldness emanated; I felt it in my fingers and toes. The passage ceiling was low. I'd have to crouch. "Please come out," I said, my voice echoing. I didn't know what else to say. I didn't want to scare them; I'd never find out who they really were then. "It's not safe here."

After waiting some minutes for a response, it was clear the children wouldn't be coming up, so I made my way slowly down the curved steps. The ceiling was low to begin with, and seemed to descend lower all the time. I've never been claustrophobic, but this increasingly tightening space was starting to make my whole body tense and my heart beat faster. A cold sweat had gathered on my neck and back, making my clothes stick.

I inched into the darkness, feeling the damp stone wall with one hand, gripping my phone in the other. At last, and many metres later, the steps came to an end, and the passage opened to a rectangular room: a crypt. There was a smell of burning. Candles, or incense. The air was heavy. Deep alcoves ate into the walls, where I imagined coffins were stored. I knew I shouldn't be there. The air itself felt oppressive. The whole place felt unwelcoming.

As I scanned the room, I saw the hem of the girl's dress as she slipped through a narrow archway: it was so quick, I'd barely even registered it. But her soft laughter confirmed her presence.

"Hey!" I called, my voice echoing around the crypt. When there was no response, I hurried forwards, my eyes focused on the narrow arch.

I turned my body sideways and edged my way through the tight space, my jacket brushing the walls. My heart pounded in my chest, hammering against my ribcage. There wasn't enough space to take a deep breath, so I held it in as long as my lungs would allow. Finally, I emerged on the other side and gasped for air.

I'd felt it first, an instinct. Then I saw a figure standing in the corner; a dark, tall mass. A long coat fell all the way to the ground, covering their shoes. They wore a hat, the brim low. A familiar sight to me now. I couldn't tell if they were facing me, or were turned away, as their face was hidden in shadow.

I stood, unable to speak. My eyes were fixed on the figure, unblinking. They didn't move. I didn't hear any breathing. They were completely still.

I noticed the ground around the figure was black, or wet, and as my eyes adjusted to the dark, I saw water streaming down his coat, dripping from his hat's brim. I felt the hairs rising on my arms. My heart drummed in my ears. My eyes were peeled for any slight movement. My whole body was on edge.

Ready.

Waiting.

His arm started to rise slowly. Could it be *him?* Again? A

shudder ran down my spine.

Jim?

I took a step back, feeling for the narrow space behind me, terrified he would grab my arm before I made it to the other side. Locating the opening, I pushed myself through as far as I could, until something snagged my jacket.

I was stuck. I couldn't budge. I couldn't even reach to pull it loose. Mustering as much strength as I could, I tried to push myself free. I heard a stone come loose and fall to the ground. Suddenly I burst onto the floor on the other side, where I entered, falling to my knees. My phone slipped from my hand, landing with a crack on the other side of the room.

The phone blinked.

Then darkness.

I got to my knees and crawled along the ground, my arms outstretched, my hands patting the rough surface for my phone. *It could have landed in one of the alcoves.* The thought of crawling into those deep recesses was overwhelming, but I had no other option. I'd never find the steps without some light.

I continued crawling, hoping to see the phone blink. Suddenly, my head knocked into something hard. Stretching my arms out, I determined it was the wall.

Trying to ignore the dull throbbing behind my forehead, I edged my way along the wall. My heart continued to hammer, and cold sweat ran down my face and back. I was terrified, knowing I wasn't alone down there.

Searching with the tip of my shoe, I found a hard step. As I eased myself up onto it, something tugged my jacket. I slipped, my knee cracking against the hard stone, and roared in pain.

Then I heard his deep, gurgled laugh, followed by the laughter of children.

I yelled up the passage, hoping someone visiting the graveyard would hear me, no matter how unlikely that might be. All I heard was their laughter over my voice. I slipped out of my jacket sleeves and planted my arms on the steps, using my good leg to push myself up. But no matter how much I pushed, some force behind me seemed to pull my body, dragging me back down into the crypt. I yelled until my throat became sore. At some point I realised all I could hear was my own yelling, and then I found I was able to climb more freely again. Finally, I saw light ahead.

"Help!" I shouted. Strangely, the daylight seemed to be fading, as if night was quickly falling. How could that be? It was only afternoon.

I stumbled out into the entrance hall. I was shocked to find that a thick mist had descended, covering every inch of the abbey, which explained the sudden darkness. I pulled myself onto my good leg. The exit from the abbey was completely blocked. I had to persevere, get far away from that crypt.

I hopped as quickly as I could, determined to keep moving forwards. I had to grapple blind for the wall for support. Then I heard the children's laughter again, just behind me, but I told myself not to look back – not that I would have seen anything due to the fog. It was then, as the exit escaped me, and the children's laughter grew louder, that a paralysing horror descended upon me: the realisation that I may never get out. My breath quickened, and I gulped mouthful after mouthful of thick, dank fog. Each breath became a struggle, until I found myself gasping, as if the very air itself contained all the souls of the graveyard, and they were trying to choke me.

I'm never going to leave, I thought. *I'm never going to see Rachel again.* The abbey, the fog, the unrelenting laughter. It was a nightmare. A nightmare from which I would never escape. Yet I stumbled on, somehow, praying to reach the exit. Inches before me, the sign appeared.

I gripped the wall to clamber through the archway and peered out into the graveyard. To my dismay, the fog was just as thick outside the abbey as it was inside it. I strained my eyes, but I couldn't see a thing before me, not even a headstone. When I held out an arm, I was shocked to find it swallowed by the fog. The paralysing despair returned again, and I wondered how it would be possible for me to make it out of the graveyard with a shattered knee and eyes blinded by the fog.

I rested against a headstone, gasping for breath. At least the children's laughter had ceased, or else the fog was so thick it silenced the sound. Even my good leg felt weak, and the thought of curling up against a headstone to sleep was beyond welcoming. My chest made a wheezing sound with each breath as I tried to swallow the thick air. I heard it rattle. There was something strange in the fog itself. It wasn't natural. It wasn't normal. Every breath was like a mouthful of toxic smoke, suffocating my lungs. I knew I didn't have much time left.

I managed to push myself from headstone to headstone. I almost tumbled as I hopped uncontrollably down the slope to the new graveyard, gathering speed. I couldn't stop myself, so I grasped helplessly for a branch, or anything, to cling onto. As I descended rapidly, I glimpsed two figures standing in front of me, right in my path.

Realising we were about to collide, I hopped onto my other leg. My knee exploded in pain before my leg gave way, and I tumbled through the grass. When I thought the pain couldn't get any worse, my head smashed into something hard. Instantly I felt woozy, as the pain erupted in the side of my head, shooting down my spine, making my body shudder.

My vision began to darken, as if the thick fog had seeped into my skull, impairing my sight. The pain from my knee and my head was too much to bear. And still I found myself staring at a headstone smeared with blood, and a name etched into the stone:

Rachel Kelly

△

Sometimes, when I'm not sleeping, I hear his footsteps outside in the hall. They're like echoes, a faint *clip-clap, clip-clap*, coming up the corridor. So faint. But he never comes through the door. Instead, he waits, and waits. Never enters. Just lingers. And then, after some hours, I hear the footsteps fading.

I can get to sleep when I take what the nurses give me. But I don't want to. I'd rather listen out for Jim. Can you believe it? I'd actually prefer to see Jim. I'd prefer to see him in this ward, standing over me, a canister in hand. Do you know why? Because I deserve it. I deserve to fucking die. And because I can't stand it. I can't stand seeing the fire. Always replaying in my mind. Every time I sleep. I'd do anything not to see it. I've begged Jim. I've fucking begged him to kill me. But he won't. He knows, and I actually think he enjoys it.

There's no Jim in my dreams. No children. It's awful. And every single night. At first, I think I've made it back to London. I find myself awake in our little flat. It's dark. Everything looks hazy. I wipe my eyes and check the clock: always displaying the digits 02:20. Rach is lying beside me, to my relief. Her back is turned to me, her head nestled in her silky, dark hair. I hear her soft breathing, almost a snore. It comforts me, momentarily. Then I hear the screams. I look around to find the room even hazier, as if a mist has seeped underneath the door.

I cough, making Rachel shudder.

"Rick?" she whispers.

The screams grow louder; they seem to be all around us, above and below. I can hear feet pounding. Alarms are ringing. Children are crying. My body freezes. I can't move a muscle. I can't even blink.

Rachel is stirring next to me, rubbing at her eyes. "What's that noise?" she asks, sitting up and yawning. "And that sme—" she begins, before breaking into a cough. She grabs my arm, shaking it madly. "Rick," she screams, then covers her mouth with her arm.

She grabs her phone, pounding the screen. "Yes," she says into it. "Fifth floor," she answers in a trembling voice.

I can hear banging on doors above. Then a bang on our door. Sirens scream outside.

"Okay," Rachel gasps, and slips out of the bed. "Stay put, okay?"

She rushes through the smoke and shuts the bedroom door. I watch as she picks up clothes, blankets, pillows, and pushes them against the bottom. She crosses to the window and throws it open. That's when I hear the voices. "Stay put," they shout. "Stay inside."

"We need to get out," I say.

"What?" Rachel asks. Her eyes are red and wide with fear.

"We need to leave," I say, louder.

"But they said to stay put. They'll come for us."

I can still hear doors banging.

People screaming.

Running.

"People are leaving," I say.

"But they're coming," Rachel protests, turning to face the window.

"We have to go," I urge, pulling away the bedsheets.

"I'm staying," Rachel says. "They're telling us to stay."

I turn around; she's still looking out of the window, gazing down. Tiny specks of fire rain outside.

"Rach," I say.

She doesn't move. The room becomes cloudier, Rachel's figure hazier. I can't tell if she's facing me or if she's turned away; her head is obscured by smoke.

"I'll come back," I say as I grab my jacket.

Smoke rapidly fills the room. There isn't much time. Smoke swirls around me. Sometimes it's black, other times a dirty brown. I'm closer and closer to waking, or dying. I don't know what's real at this stage. I just know I have to leave. Find help. Come back for Rachel. Always come back for Rachel.

I'm running from the room, running from her. But I can't see. Everything is white. All I can hear are children screaming. I keep running, rushing through smoke. I think I'm in Heaven. I think I've died. I see two small children standing in the smoke. I run towards them, grabbing each of them by an arm.

There are flames. White hot flames.

It's not Heaven, I realise. I can't find a way out.

My skin burns. Black smoke engulfs me. It's hell.

And then I wake up.

XVI

Rachel, 2018

Transcript of 999 call

Date: Wednesday, October 31, 2018 02:30 AM

Operator: Hello, fire brigade.

Caller: Hi, yes, it's me again.

Operator: You're still in the flat?

Caller: Yes.

Operator: We've got a fire engine already there dealing with it, okay?

Caller: Yes, you're here but I'm still stuck on the fifth floor and I don't know how to get out.

Operator: The fire is on the first floor so you're well away from the fire.

Caller: No, I'm not, there's smoke coming through the door.

Operator: There's smoke coming through?

Caller: Yes, the fire must be on my floor now.

Operator: Can you close any doors to stop the smoke coming through?

Caller: Yes, I already have, we already have.

Operator: Can you stop the smoke coming into the flat using any blankets, any towels, or something?

Caller: We did, we have.

Operator: You need to close your doors and windows, okay?

Caller: Okay, is that good? I need to keep the window open. The smoke is coming in.

Operator: Right, if the smoke is coming in. Um. Okay. If you open a window and it's letting the smoke out, you can leave it open, okay?

Caller: Okay.

Operator: But if smoke is coming in through the window, you need to close it.

Caller: It's open. How do I get out?

Operator: Which flat are you in?

Caller: 20, but it's just me. My boyfriend has just left.

Operator: Okay, just cover any smoke. The best thing for you to do is to stay where you are. I will pass a message to the crew outside to say that you're in your flat, number 20 on the fifth floor (over speaking) —

[sound of alarms]

Caller: The alarms are going.

Operator: They will. I can hear them.

Caller: (coughing) Please come. Please.

Operator: Is there fire?

Caller: The fire's coming in.

Operator: Okay, madam, are you able to stop the fire coming into the flat?

Caller: It's coming through the door. I have to (coughing). I've got to put the phone, I've got to put the phone — it's coming in.

Operator: Hello? We'll get someone up to help you. Hello?

Caller: (inaudible whispering)

Operator: I will.

Caller: (inaudible)

Operator: You're welcome.

Caller: (inaudible)

Operator: I'll tell him. It's okay. I'll tell him. I'll tell him. Message on four, fire on the fifth floor as well. Hello? Operator, is this line open?

XVII

Pierce, 2020

Email from Pierce Rowlandson to Julia Crouch

From: pierce rowlandson <pierce.rowlandson@caxtonpub-lishing.com>
Sent: Wednesday, January 1, 2020 08:35 PM
To: Julia.crouch@caxtonpublishing.com
Subject: Rick

Julia,

You won't believe where I am – Brian's cottage!

It's exactly how Rick had described: a small, rustic kitchen, and a living room opposite with a fireplace and basket of turf. Quite a nice place Brian keeps. So it's safe to conclude the cottage exists. But there's no fog or mist, or ghosts across the lake. I just hope Jim Harrow doesn't come knocking ;)

I wasn't the only visitor at the hospital. Brian appeared in a panic just as I was leaving, all flushed and gasping for breath. He's portlier than Rick had described. Maybe it's all the brandy.

Anyway, before I get to that, Rick practically gave the notepad back to me. I mean, he didn't resist. So I have it. As well as the full MS and letters. He did try to hold onto my pen though; not sure why. I tried to retrieve it gently, but it was wedged between his finger and thumb. I hadn't noticed just how ravaged his hands were. He seemed to always wear gloves or cover them with his sleeves. But I could see the burns, still red raw. Some of the skin was missing from his fingers, making them appear even longer than they actually were, almost claw-like. I had to yank my pen from his grip in the end.

I bumped into Brian in the corridor on the way out. I recognized the tweed jacket and trilby hat. He looked older than me, maybe late sixties, but he might easily have been a strapping young man once.

"Is he alright?" he panted.

"He's resting," I said, keeping my back against the glass window of the door, paranoid that Rick would somehow communicate what I'd taken. "Perhaps best to come back tomorrow." His mouth opened as if he was going to say something, but no words came out. "I'm sure you can leave that with the staff," I suggested, nodding at the plastic bag in his hand, packed with biscuits, bananas and other items. I could make out a small bottle, possibly brandy. I rather admired their friendship. "How did you find out?" I asked, hoping to stall him.

"I've been trying to get through to Rick's phone for days," he said. "Honestly, I'd thought he'd gone back to London. I emailed, and still nothing." He took a deep breath. "I thought I'd check with the airport, to see if he'd returned the car. They said it had been returned, but no Rick. They said there was some kind of accident? I've been on a wild goose chase since. How is he? Are you sure I can't go in?"

"He's resting," I repeated. "He needs to rest his head. Looks like he's had a nasty head injury."

To my surprise, he asked if I needed a place to stay. I had Bed & Breakfast booked in Ballinasloe, but I didn't tell Brian that. It was too tempting to see where Rick had stayed. At first, I thought the cottage might be fictional, but now I was being given the opportunity to stay there myself. He seemed pleased when I'd accepted and even said I could stay there for the weekend, as January's a quiet month for him. I offered to pay but he refused.

"I suppose I'd better leave this with a nurse," he said, holding out the bag.

"Yes, I'm sure I saw a desk this way."

Before we left, I looked around to see if Rick had fallen asleep. I was surprised to see he was sitting upright, gazing out of the window. The scars on his face seemed brighter, almost burning. He was frowning, his eyes squinting, as if he'd spotted something just outside the window.

What's he looking at? I wondered. Or was he just staring at his own mangled reflection?

"Everything alright?" Brian asked.

I reassured Brian that it was, and then led him to the desk in the hall, keeping an eye out for the nurse who'd phoned me. After dropping off the bag off, I was eager to get out of the hospital, afraid that Brian would suspect something in my bag.

I drove along behind Brian out of Ballinasloe town, all the way to the cottage, where a bottle of brandy was waiting for me on the kitchen counter. I offered Brian a glass, but he said he was exhausted after searching for Rick, and wanted an early night. He did suggest I head to Castlestrange Lodge and try their stew, but I doubt they're still serving at this hour. It's worth a look. Besides, it'll be another location fact-checked off my list. I wonder if this 'weejee' board is still there. See how much I put into this job, even during holidays. I think I'll take the car though.

I realise I promised to send a summary of Rick's MS, but I'm far too curious about this pub. Plus, my stomach's growling. And you probably won't see these emails until Monday. I'll send it tomorrow though, while it's fresh in my head.

Kind regards,

Pierce

PS there was no sign of my nurse :'(

△

From: pierce rowlandson <pierce.rowlandson@caxtonpublishing.com>
Sent: Sunday, January 5, 2020 1:05 PM
To: julia.crouch@caxtonpublishing.com
Subject: Rick

Julia,

Rick's dead.

My phone rang while I was queuing at the airport. I was surprised to hear, at long last, the voice of the nurse who'd originally phoned me. I must admit, I wasn't expecting the phone call.

"What happened?" I asked.

"He's deteriorated," the nurse said.

"He's what?" I said loudly, getting some looks from the other passengers in the queue. "What does that mean?"

"It's probably best to tell you in person."

"Tell me now."

"Okay," he said, before his voice dropped to a whisper. "We think he fell from his window. Or jumped. It happened last night, in the early hours of the morning. We heard him scream, so it could have been an accident. Does he have any mental health history, do you know?"

"I don't know," I said. "He lost his girlfriend over a year ago. Probably."

"Anyway, I just thought I'd let you know before you left, in case you wanted to stay."

"Of course," I said. I wondered if I should stay. I could work from the B&B in Ballinasloe (I'd rather not stay at Brian's cottage any longer – I'll explain everything tomorrow!). "Are you there today?" I asked him.

"Yes, like every other day this week," he said.

"Really? I didn't see you there."

"Mr Rowlandson, I'm Rick's nurse. I've been looking after

him since he arrived."

This confused me. The only nurses I saw were female. Not the young nurse with the clipboard? She sounded so different on the phone. Bloody phones!

Of course, I didn't stay – and not because of this mix-up! I just wanted to get back to London, back to Shirley, and I'd rather not bump into Brian again. I've kept Rick's work close. And I'm eager to deliver it safely to the office.

I'm just after landing, and thought I'd send you this email with the news. I must inform HR first thing Monday morning. Golly, it must have been a terrible way to die. Would anyone attend the funeral, apart from Brian? Poor chap.

I skimmed through my notepad and the letters on the plane. Rick's ending was sufficient, but the dream could be cut, I think. Better to end it with the headstone reveal. No one needed to know how Rachel died exactly. Keep it ambiguous. All it needs is a title. I scribbled some ideas on a new page: *The Harrow Haunt, The Harrow Curse*, among others. I'm sure marketing will come up with a better, more commercial title.

I'll focus on writing up the summary this evening, after I pick up Shirley from the neighbour.

Kind regards,

Pierce

PS isn't it strange how they both jumped?

EMAIL FROM PIERCE ROWLANDSON TO JULIA CROUCH

△

From: pierce rowlandson <pierce.rowlandson@caxtonpublishing.com>
Sent: Monday, January 6, 2020 02:21 AM
To: julia.crouch@caxtonpublishing.com
Subject: Rick

Julia,

Finally writing from home now. Shirley's asleep in my lap. I've spent tonight re-reading Rick's MS, my notepad with his ending and the letters. I'm attaching the summary here. It's much later than I realised but I got a little waylaid. Not with Shirley. Something odd happened. Sometime around midnight.

While I was sitting here in my upstairs office, writing the summary, I heard a thump from downstairs. I ignored it, convincing myself it was in my head; I had just surmised Rick's account of hearing footsteps in the cottage. But then I heard it again. A dull thump.

It sounded like it was coming from the stairs. I went to check. I couldn't see anyone, or anything. I turned on the hall light. Still nothing. I headed down in any case, to double check the door was still locked. It was. What had caused the thump, then?

I went to check on Shirley, thinking she'd knocked something over, but she was snuggled up in her little bed, purring away. I yearned to pick her up and carry her with me, craving her warmth, but decided not to disturb her sleep.

That's when I saw something glimmering on the floor, between the front door and the foot of the stairs. I got down on my hunkers, peering. It looked like a shoe track. From one of my own shoes, probably. I'd taken them off after coming inside.

I headed back upstairs, telling myself I just needed to sleep. I've had too many sleepless nights lately. Rick's story, and that place. That board. It's messing with my head. I had an early start this morning. Maybe that's why I think I'm hearing things. I just need to sleep. It'll be a long day tomorrow. Meetings with HR. Sharing this book. I'll be dying for a coffee no doubt.

There it is again, that thump. I hear it when I start writing. It stops when I stop. Starts when I start. There it is again. Thump. Like a boot. It sounds like it's coming from the stairs. And not just one, but two thumps. It's coming up the stairs, Julia. I'm going to have to go. I'm going to phone the police. But what can I say? I'm hearing sounds? I can hear boots? I don't even know for certain if there's a person out there. I can't see. Wait. There's a shadow. It's moving. They're coming up the stairs. They're coming closer.

Clip, clap, it comes. Clip, clap.

I have to go. I have to phone the police.

Pierce Rowlandson
Commissioning Editor
ScaryBooks
Caxton & Co Publishing
Email: pierce.rowlandson@caxtonpublishing.com

This message and any attachments are solely for the intended recipient. Any views or opinions expressed are solely those of the author and do not necessarily represent those of Caxton & Co Publishing. If you are not the intended recipient, disclosure, copying, use or distribution of the information included in this message is prohibited. Please immediately and permanently delete. Company registered in England.

Transcript of 999 call

Date: Monday, January 6, 2020 02:22 AM

Operator: Met Police, what's your emergency?

Caller: There's someone outside my study.

Operator: There's someone outside your study?

Caller: Yes, I'm at home. They've broken in and now they're on the landing. Just, please come.

Operator: What's your name and address?

Caller: Pierce Rowlandson. (Gives address). Can they come now please?

Operator: What's your postcode?

Caller: (Gives postcode). Please, please hurry. I can see their shadow.

Operator: I'm assigning two officers just now. Are you on

your own, sir?

Caller: Yes, it's just me and Shirley. But Shirley's downstairs.

Operator: Is Shirley your wife?

Caller: No, no, she's my cat.

Operator: Are you hurt?

Caller: No, I'm at my desk.

Operator: Tell me what's happening.

Caller: I can just see their shadow under the door. I can hear the floor creak.

Operator: Is the door locked?

Caller: No, I don't—

Operator: Can you go lock the door?

Caller: I can't, they're just there.

Operator: Do you know who's there?

Caller: No, I heard them before though.

Operator: Please lock the door. When did you hear them before?

Caller: Around midnight, I think. I heard them downstairs and went to look.

Operator: Did you see who they were?

Caller: No, I can only see their shadow. But they've stopped. They're standing on the landing, outside my door. I'm shaking, oh please get them here now.

Operator: Two officers in the locality are already on their way. It shouldn't be more than five minutes. Make sure the door is locked.

Caller: They're moving. The shadow's moving.

Operator: Have you locked the door?

Caller: I'm making my way over now.

Operator: Stay on the line, sir. Is the door locked?

Caller: The handle's moving. I should've locked the door, like Rick did.

Operator: Who's Rick?

Caller: He's just an author. He died. But—

Operator: The officers will be there any moment now.

[creaking sound]

Caller: The door's opening. There's someone there.

Operator: Can you see who it is?

Caller: He's standing there. But he's wearing a hat, I can't see who it is...

Operator: Stay on the line, sir. Can you describe the man?

Caller: He's tall, thin. He's wearing a coat and, and, there's something in his hand.

Operator: Is he carrying a weapon?

Caller: He's holding a canister. A large canister.

[loud bang]

Operator: What was that sound?

Caller: He's dropped it. It's spilling everywhere.

Operator: What's spilling?

Caller: It's dark. Oil, or something. It's all over the carpet.

Operator: Is there anywhere you can run? Is there another door you can use?

Caller: There's just the window. He's looking for something. I don't understand.

Operator: You need to get out. Is it safe to use the window?

Caller: I can't, I'm upstairs. His hands are white. Scarred. He's pulling out a match.

Operator: Please move to the window. I'll keep an officer outside.

Caller: He's fiddling with a box. A match.

Operator: There's an officer outside the window.

[bang in distance]

Operator: The officers are here.

Caller: I see him. His face. Oh God, it's his face. It's burned. I can see his scars.

Operator: Tell me who it is, sir.

Caller: It can't be him. No, please, not again. It can't be. But it is him. It is him. And he's looking directly at me.

[sound of a match scratching]

Caller: (inaudible)

Operator: Hello? Hello, the officers are coming up, okay? Hello? Hello? Hello?

Acknowledgements

'A Man from England Named Robert Harrow' is a retelling of 'The Fairies' Revenge' from *Ancient Legends, Mystic Charms, and Superstitions of Ireland* (1888) by Lady Jane Francesca Agnes Wilde, a collection of stories obtained from a variety of sources including oral communication, contributions from her husband, Sir William Wilde, a prominent Irish folklorist, and her own observations. It was proclaimed a 'valuable addition to the literature of folk-lore and mythology; taken down, for the most part, from oral communications with the [Irish] peasantry,' *Scotsman* (Project Gutenberg, 2020. Web. 19 Nov. 2023). William Wilde, the father of Oscar Wilde, was born in County Roscommon, Ireland, where much of *The Weejee Man* draws inspiration.

Ouija Gone Wild: Shocking True Stories (2012) by Rosemary Ellen Guiley and Rick Fisher and *Collecting Ouija Boards in the UK* (2019) by Alan Tigwell are two great books if you want to learn more about spirit boards. And, of course, there is *A History of Spiritualism* (1926) by Arthur Conan Doyle about the movement in general. Special thanks to Alan Tigwell's book however for introducing me to a range of fascinating names and terms for spirit boards including 'Wee-Ja board', 'We-ja girl', 'Witch board', 'Witchity board', 'Weed-ja', 'Magii board', 'Bowieja' and many more!

Thank you to members and friends of the **Horror Writers Association** for answering my random questions about trademarks, when to include content warnings and much more. Also special thanks to The Gothic Bookshelf, a welcoming and encouraging space for writers of horror and the gothic.

Thank you to my little group of avid readers: Sean Sweeney, for injecting some extra drama where it was needed, Ciara Lally for being my undercover nurse, and Emma Buckingham for the encouragement to publish the book.